Mister Hockey

Also by Lia Riley

Mister Hockey

HELLIONS ANGELS

LIA RILEY

AVONIMPULSE
An Imprint of HarperCollinsPublishers

This book is a work of fiction. References to real people, events, establishments, organizations, or locales are intended only to provide a sense of authenticity, and are used fictitiously. All other characters, and all incidents and dialogue, are drawn from the author's imagination and are not to be construed as real.

MISTER HOCKEY. Copyright © 2017 by Lia Riley. All rights reserved. Printed in the United States of America. No part of this book may be used or reproduced in any manner whatsoever without written permission except in the case of brief quotations embodied in critical articles and reviews. For information, address HarperCollins Publishers, 195 Broadway, New York, NY 10007.

Digital Edition JULY 2017 ISBN: 978–0–062662460
Print Edition ISBN: 978–0–062662477

Cover design by Nadine Badalaty
Cover photograph © El Nariz / Shutterstock

Avon Impulse and the Avon Impulse logo are registered trademarks of HarperCollins Publishers in the United States of America.

Avon and HarperCollins are registered trademarks of HarperCollins Publishers in the United States of America and other countries.

FIRST EDITION

17 18 19 20 21 HDC 10 9 8 7 6 5 4 3 2 1

To Jarah, you ARE a gift and I love you so much

Acknowledgments

I WOULD LIKE to express my gratitude to all the people who made this book possible. To Elle Keck who was a wise, thorough and thoughtful editor; to Emily Sylvan Kim who is the most amazing agent ever; to my writing family: Jennifer Blackwood, Jennifer Ryan, Chanel Cleeton, A.J Pine, Jules Barnard, Natalie Blitt and Megan Erickson; and my real family who deserves all the clean laundry and hot meals . . . someday.

Mister Hockey

Chapter One

JED WEST'S STOMACH curdled faster than overheated hollandaise sauce as he squinted at the menu for Zachary's, Denver's popular all-day breakfast hangout. Ghost-like shadows haunted the specials list, blurring the descriptions for peanut butter French toast, country fried steak benedict and sweet potato pancakes. Ah, shit. Not fucking *now*. There went the prices too—the dollar signs and numbers blurring until barely legible.

No point blinking. He knew the drill. Jaw tight, he reached for his orange juice, took a swig and waited. Short bouts of double vision had dogged him ever since game seven, the pattern the same. After a minute or two, his focus would snap back to normal as if nothing had happened. Until then, he needed to follow one of Coach's favorite axioms: Suck it up, buttercup.

Who cared about the damn menu anyway? He

pushed it to one side, having already ordered the "Hunger Blaster," chorizo and eggs smashed between a jalapeño cheddar biscuit—the kind of breakfast that wanted to kill you in the best kind of ways—and crunched ice. Too bad the cubes didn't pass on their chill, because this . . . situation for lack of a better word, was getting under his skin and it shouldn't.

No—scratch that. It *couldn't.*

Unexplained double vision wasn't a walk in the park, but facts were facts. And the ugly truth was that if he didn't quit batting his lashes like Scarlett O'Hara with a fly in her skirt, *The Post*'s toughest sports columnist would glance up from across the table, mistake his tic for a cheesedick wink, and go *Lord of the Flies* on his nut sack.

At least for the moment, Neve Angel was occupied. She hunched over her digital voice recorder, dark bangs obscuring her sharp gaze as she fiddled with the control settings. Her lips moved to the upbeat Buddy Holly song piping over the sound system while she plucked a mic from her messenger bag. His vision came back online in time for him to read the orange button pinned to the front.

Had a Ball at The Rock Creek Testicle Festival.

Christ, looked to be an authentic souvenir too.

Slamming his knees together, he forced a grin, the one that had potential endorsements lined up around the block, eager for him to shill everything from vitamin-infused coconut water to shaving cream. He unwrapped the paper napkin from around the fork and knife, and began tearing the corner into neat strips.

No doubt the eye thing was fatigue-related, an inevitable toll from the grueling NHL season and subsequent hard-fought playoffs. Everything would be all right in the end. If it wasn't all right, it wasn't the end.

"You plan on telling me what's up with Mount Napkin Shreds?" Neve leaned her elbows on the recycled wood tabletop, a signal they were shifting into interview mode. Her brows arched beneath her thick-cut bangs. "Nervous about being in the hot seat, princess?"

"Yeah, terrified," he answered laconically, not missing a beat. Hiding his true feelings behind a mask of confidence was a reflex; it came with the territory of having the C stitched on the front of his jersey. A good captain never showed fear to an opponent. "A jackal's bark is worse than its bite."

"Jackal? Don't tell me you're using Gunnarisms now." She rolled her eyes. "And I'd so wanted to enjoy my bagel without gagging."

The Hellions head coach, Tor Gunnar, had a reputation for dismissing the press as "jackals." He fostered a tense relationship with journalists, in particular, the tiny woman sitting opposite. Neve had run a piece on his divorce a few years ago. He retaliated by refusing to call on her during press conferences. Neve hit back with increasingly critical op-eds. Their mutual enmity had devolved to the stuff of local legend.

"Big words, but don't you and Coach G have a love-to-hate thing going?" Jed teased, "Could be masking some serious sexual tension, you should look into that. Plus if he got laid, he might smile more than once a year. The whole team would owe you one."

"Hmm," Neve mused into her glass. "How many of these ice cubes could fit up your nose? Hard to say. My money is on ten. Five up each nostril."

He chuckled, sliding one of his arms over the back of the leather booth. A busser clearing a nearby table caught his idle glance and the top plate slammed against her chest, smearing ketchup over her white blouse.

Jed pretended not to notice her flustered screech and instead focused on a framed poster that read A Yawn is a Silent Scream for Coffee. It never stopped being weird, even after all this time, to be *that* guy. The one who got the second look, the screams from the fans, slipped numbers scrawled on a bar napkin every time he went out for a beer. A few times a year, push-up bras came in the mail.

When he landed on *Cosmo*'s Sexiest Men in Sport list last year, the guys on the team had given him a world of shit. "Miiiiiiister Hockey," they'd catcall in the locker room, using the nickname from the article. "Strike a pose. Come on, man, do your best Blue Steel."

Not that female attention was bad. It was just that he woke up each morning and put on pants one leg at a time. He liked his job and was damn good at doing it, but it wasn't pulling kids from burning buildings or defending his country. Hero worship could mess with a guy's mind. Make him think he was invincible. And he'd seen firsthand where that kind of mentality could land an athlete.

He massaged his left temple in a slow circle. Nowhere good.

"There's a story behind that frown." Neve batted a lemon slice around her glass. "Should we start there?"

"I have resting bitch face." He refused to back down from her narrow-eyed scrutiny. Counted to ten. *Four . . . five . . . six . . .*

"Nope. Normally you're grinning like a monkey with a new banana," she shot back.

"Never got into bananas." He gave a one-shouldered shrug. "More of a berry fan."

"Fine. Have it your way." Neve ran out the clock with her usual tenacity. "Stay mysterious."

"Hey now. I'm serious." He raked a hand through his hair, a subtle way to show off his championship ring. "Everything's good in my world. Great even."

Yup. Except for the fact that he'd spent the morning in the Hellions screening room, poring over tapes from the final minutes of game seven. He'd taken a lead pass and skated into the Detroit zone. Score tied, adrenaline was high. Must have been the reason the Red Wings D-man sent the business end of his stick into Jed's right eye socket.

Jed had watched himself up on the flat screen push himself off the ice and wave away medical attention. It was surreal, like watching a movie about someone else's life. He couldn't remember a damn thing about those few minutes, but it appeared that even his lizard brain had an aversion to getting benched.

The hit hadn't been enough to fuck him though, right?

"All right, all right. Enough monkeying around, *now* you really are on record." Neve clicked the red record button. Her voice dropped a half octave and took on a more formal affectation, as if she had morphed into a National Public Radio host. "Hello and welcome to another edition of *Sports Heaven*, with me, Neve, Denver's favorite Angel," she purred. "Today I'm lucky enough to be sitting down with Jed West, captain of the Denver Hellions. Thanks for chatting, Westy."

"Pleasure's mine." He drawled, lifting his empty pint glass in cheers, shoving the tapes to the hamper in the back of his mind.

"Since getting traded from the Sharks, you've taken the Hellions all the way twice. Broken one of the longest losing streaks in NHL history and—"

The raucous chorus to the song "All I Do is Win," emanated from inside her blouse. "Shoot. Hang on." She hit Pause and fished her phone from the gap in her shirt.

"That's one hell of a phone holder," he deadpanned.

"Hush." Her small mouth went mulish. "A bra is a modern gal's Swiss army knife. Now. Where was I?" She hit Play and steepled her fingers. "Ah, yes, the Westy magic. What's your secret?"

"I don't know. The usual." He grabbed a napkin shred from the pile in front of him and rolled the thin paper into a neat ball. "It's like this, see . . . on full moons I lure a goat onto the ice, preferably a young one. Too old and they get ornery. There's chanting. Followed by a naked drum circle. Then the ritual sacrifice complete with a—"

"All I Do is Win" blared again.

Neve ripped the phone from her cleavage and frowned at the screen. "It's my sister. Breezy never calls during a workday. I've got to take this." She clicked off the recorder and slammed the phone to her ear. "What's wrong?" Two lines dented the skin between her brows. "Okay. Stop. Slow down, way, way down. Breathe. No. That's hysterical laughter bordering on tears. I want breaths, deep ones from your diaphragm. Warmer. Warmer . . . better." She gave a grim nod. "Uh-huh, uh-huh. Yep. No, he didn't! I don't care a fig if it *is* the weather. I've always said he's asshat. Me? Hmm." She drummed her fingers, shooting him a considered look. "Got plans for the afternoon?"

"Dunno." Jed shrugged, not loving the gleam in her eye. "Getting interviewed by you, then going to lift at the gym." *Or commencing an online search for a discreet neurologist.* "Why?"

"Tor Gunnar was booked to headline a kiddie literacy event at the Rosedale Branch Library." She pronounced the Hellion coach's name the same way a *Harry Potter* character might curse Voldemort. Taking a swig of ice tea, as if to cleanse the name from her palate, she continued. "He had a charity golf event in Scottsdale and there's been a weather delay with the airlines. The same crappy system dumping all the rain here is causing flash floods there. His flight's canceled and that leaves my little sis stuck as a Head Children's Librarian with no special guest and a community room filling with starry-eyed young hockey fans—"

"Your sister's name is *Breezy*?"

"Briana." Neve smirked. "But I couldn't pronounce it when I was little and my version stuck. Anyway, she's asking me to step in as the surprise special guest, but seeing as *you're* here . . ."

He got the hint. "You need a volunteer?"

"Why, I declare! What a wonderful, generous offer." Her exaggerated coo faded back to her usual brisk tone. "Here's the deal. I love two things in this world: my job and my family. I'm telling you, Breezy performs bona fide miracles at that library. Letting down those rug rats would kill her. And besides . . ." She drummed her nails on the table's veneer again with a smug look.

"What?" He crossed his arms, as if the gesture could hide the jealous flame that flared every time he was presented with evidence of other people's normal, happy family lives.

"Nothing." She wiped a hand over her mouth, erasing the mysterious smirk. "So . . . what's it going to be?

Will you heed the urgent call of a damsel in distress? Just remember that if the answer is no, then the topic of my next podcast is going to be about hockey captains who devastate local fans by refusing to support worthwhile community events."

He threw up his hands in mock annoyance. "I'd have said yes. No need to stoop to Tony Soprano threats." For all her smart talk, he enjoyed Neve's company. He didn't have a sister, but if he did, he'd wish for one like her.

"Nice to find out that your good-guy attitude isn't an act." The tension lines bracketing her mouth vanished as she gave him an honest grin. "You'd be surprised how often celebrity athletes suck donkey balls." She shoved the phone back to her ear. "Breezy? Crisis averted. The cavalry's coming."

"Your order is coming out in just a minute." The waitress bustled to the table and leaned in close. A clump of mascara dangled off the edge of her lashes. "Want anything else in the meantime? More fresh squeezed orange juice . . . my phone number?"

"Oy! That's enough of that." Neve stuffed her phone back down her shirt. "We need that breakfast sandwich and bagel to go." She began packing her things in quick efficient movements as the waitress retreated. "Follow me over?"

"I know the way." His condo wasn't far from the Rosedale library. "Speer Boulevard, hop off on Tenth?"

He rose and grabbed his Gore-Tex jacket. "What's the plan?"

"You'll say a few words, something short." Neve shrugged as she stood and strode toward the front door, accepting the brown bags from the waitress and passing him one before paying the bill. "You know the drill. 'School is cool' and 'Reading is for winners' feel-good stuff. Wing it. Oh!" She raised a finger. "Breezy did mention that the speaker has to share their favorite picture book. You *are* literate, right?" She winked.

"Remember how I played defense for Stanford?" He opened and held the door. "I also happened to major in Finance." It took effort to keep the edge from his voice. Stereotypes were self-fulfilling prophecies and he had spent years working his ass off not to be another "dumb jock" cruising by on a subpar GPA. In truth, reading wasn't his favorite, but at least numbers always made sense.

"Finance, huh?" Neve missed his stiffness as she scooted past. "Every time I talk about banking I get withdrawal symptoms." She snorted at her corny joke. "But in all seriousness, thanks for the Good Samaritan gesture. That was cool, and Breezy's going to appreciate it more than you could imagine." Again came that hint of a private smile gone as soon as it started. "Wow, get a load of this rain. We need a snorkel and fins to cross the parking lot."

"Tell me." He tugged up his hood. "This sister with the funny name, is she anything like you?" God help

Denver if there was another mouthy Chihuahua on the loose.

"Breezy? Not in the least." Neve opened her umbrella with a flourish. "But she's my best friend. Let her down and I'll drop-kick you faster than you can say Bobby Orr."

Chapter Two

"LET'S TRY IT again. From the top." Breezy Angel sucked in, straining for the costume zipper, putting herself at risk of serious rib crackage. Who was she kidding; these loosey-goosey abs hadn't seen a decent crunch in years. They could barely flex, let alone possess the strength to break bone. Sweat prickled the nape of her neck while stars skimmed the edge of her vision. "Oof. Come on, come on," she huffed, grimacing.

She reached and almost . . . almost . . . almost . . . her fingers grazed the zipper.

Success.

She gripped the millimeter of metal and tugged. Stubborn little sucker refused to budge. Frowning, she tried again.

Same result.

At fifteen years old, the library's Super Reader costume had seen better days. But last summer it fit fine.

"Ugh." The bathroom scale had been an asshole since the Rory breakup. During last week's move to her new—and first—home of her very own, she'd exiled the spiteful hunk of metal to the garage as punishment, but it hadn't lied. Fifteen extra pounds padded her hips and butt, a result of an ongoing ménage a trois with Ben and Jerry.

Zzzzzzzerp! The zipper gave way.

"Sweet Sugar Babies!" Her voice echoed off the women's room tile as she clutched her pancaked breasts. Her nipples inverted and her naval squashed her spine, but hey, she'd stuffed herself inside—victorious, more or less.

Now to survive the next hour without laughing, sitting or breathing.

Not that she'd ever been a slender, willowy sort of gal. Her body tended to softness and a good cheese plate was better than size six jeans. She owned her juicy ass and had an allergy to any talk about how a "real" woman had a) curves b) no curves or c) hard-won muscles.

Nope. Sorry. All a so-called real woman needed to own the title was a heartbeat.

Boom. Done. End of story.

But even still, she wanted to feel good in her skin . . . and right now, she didn't. She hadn't in too long.

Picking up the Jed West coffee mug from the edge of the sink—a recent twenty-ninth birthday gift from her big sister—she drained the bitter dark roast before glancing at his photo printed on the side.

Sigh.

Westy was the carrots to her peas. The cheese to her macaroni. The gin to her tonic. The . . . the . . . corned beef to her cabbage.

Those irises were a tug of war between June grass green and hickory bark brown. How many hours had she spent trying to bestow his perfect hazel eye color with the right poetic descriptors?

Spoiler: a lot.

No regrets, because that face was a gift to humanity; as if no matter what the nightly news indicated, the world couldn't be going to hell in a handbasket if it had conspired to produce such a perfect male jaw. And those freckles. Yeah. Wow. Those freckles just weren't fair.

She checked her reflection with a half-hearted shrug, nothing much to cheer or sneer there. On a positive note, yay for a good hair day. The half beehive paired well with a low side ponytail. Straight sixties glam. She leaned closer, wiping a lipstick smudge from her lower lip. Her usual cat-eye makeup was on point too. The black liquid liner gave her wings, even as the low hum from the crowd in the community room threatened to send her heart into an Icarus death spiral.

Everyone twiddling their thumbs in the folding chairs was expecting to meet the Hellion's popular coach, Tor Gunnar, fresh from his second straight NHL championship victory, who was sidelined due to bad weather. Ugh. Bad news on a good day, a disaster when the Library Board of Trustees kept making ominous rumblings about pending cuts.

Municipal appropriations had plunged and to add insult to injury the library system had lost several hundred thousand dollars in federal funding. It wasn't a question of if there would be branch closures or department belt-tightening, but when. Her department better shine if it hoped to survive the dark days ahead.

Breezy nibbled the inside of her cheek, wincing as one bite too hard flooded her mouth with a faintly metallic taste. No way would she get flushed down the professional tubes without a fight. Her department transformed the children's zone for each holiday, made it a place where young patrons could come after school and get homework help from senior volunteers, reluctant readers were paired with the perfect book, or took part in a Lego or chess club, participated in drop-in Robotics or Minecraft, and where local parents could form connections with one another at toddler story hours or in a parenting class.

Anyone who wanted to dismiss librarians as boring bookworms had never heard Breezy rap out "I Like Big Books and I Cannot Lie" after one Jack and Diet Coke too many—bonus points for her twerking skills.

And if she ever daydreamed about opening an independent children's bookshop, well it was nothing but another of her fantasies, like the one where she met Jed West and he fell madly in love.

Here! The phone buzzed with her sister's text. Speaking of someone who lived their dreams, Neve had the perfect job for a card-carrying member of the Hellions Angels, the nickname of their family's hockey fan club. From October to April (and the playoffs, God willing), Angel women spent Hellion game nights crammed into Aunt Lo's creaky Victorian in Five Points behaving like unashamed dorks: Mom, Granny Dee, Aunt Joanie, Aunt Shell and her best friend, Margot, who was basically an honorary member of the family.

Those were the evenings when her stepdad and the uncles retreated to the man cave above the garage to shoot pool, play foosball and pout over their loss of the living room's sixty-inch flat-screen. The men were Bronco diehards to a one, obsessed with fantasy football leagues.

But the Angel women?

They were all about the puck, a tradition started with Granny Dee and proudly passed through three generations.

Some folks were obsessed with Marvel Comics or Doctor Who or Harry Potter. She self-identified as Ravenclaw, but the rest of her family didn't know the word *cosplay* or that Comic-Con existed. And yet they donned red devil horns, smeared their faces with crimson-and-white paint and brandished plastic pitchforks without a shred of embarrassment.

"Good, you're here!" Neve burst in wearing black dress pants and a gray collared shirt. Breezy loved vibrant patterns, the bolder and funkier the better while her big sister had an allergic reaction to wearing anything that wasn't a neutral color or cotton. "Your assistant thought you'd still be changing."

"Thanks for bailing me out on no notice." Breezy rinsed the Westy mug and tossed it in her "Reading is Sexy" tote bag before reaching for the door. "We're running late so here's how it's going to go up there. I'll introduce you and . . ."

"Breezy—wait!"

The nerves connecting her feet to her brain snapped midstep into the hall. She froze, her gaze raking a pair of vintage Adidas sneakers and climbed up gray sweatpants hanging off a trim, narrow waist. Shadows played on the cotton, highlighting the merest suggestion of a bulge. Then up to a broad chest and even broader shoulders. The distinctive chin. The scruffy jaw. Those eyes that were . . . that were . . . what were colors?

What was life?

Every muscle in her body flexed tight, her heart unable to squeeze anything approaching a full beat.

Holy guacamole with a side of chips.

Jed.

West.

Captain of the Hellions.

Jed West.

Her ultimate celebrity crush—Jed freaking West was in *her* library. Leaning against a cinder block wall four feet away.

Her heart paid a visit to her throat. Small hairs prickled at the nape of her neck.

No way. No freaking way. But yes. Oh yes. Oh God yes.

His black raincoat offset the rich, espresso-brown gloss to his thick hair. Tiny rain beads clung to each perfect strand, bright as carat diamonds. The Fates swooned. Nope, wait. That particularly breathless mewl came from her own parted lips.

"Told you I was bringing a surprise." Neve spoke in a slow, even cadence while her piercing gray eyes silently ordered, *Get a grip, dude. Do not lose your shit.*

"Nice cape. Do I get one?" Jed's famously lazy smile twisted an invisible screw at the apex of Breezy's thighs, a sharp twinge that settled into an acute ache. Of course he didn't know about the starring role he played in her biweekly Hitachi wand sessions. Or the imaginary dirty talk he groaned in her ear while she writhed in the dark.

I taste you on my lips, sweetheart. Tell me who owns you.

He couldn't have the first clue about her dirty overactive imagination, but Jesus H. Christopher Christ riding a unicycle, she knew. Whenever she fantasized about a guy putting ranch dressing in her Hidden Valley, he was the one wielding the big, big bottle.

Her cheeks turned a subtle shade of rose-blooming-in-hell as she forced a gasping chuckle. "Uh, hang tight. I forgot . . . a . . . thing."

Beating a quick retreat into the bathroom, she did what any non-freaking-out, red-blooded gal would do when encased in ancient threadbare red Lycra and confronted by their ultimate dream man.

She let the door smack his beautiful face.

Chapter Three

"PLEASE." BREEZY'S HORRIFIED gaze bored into the bathroom door until her eyeballs burned. "Oh please, oh please," she chanted through the fingers pressed to her mouth. Let this nightmare be an oxygen-deprived dream triggered by the too-tight costume.

A comforting flicker of hope flared in the black pit of her belly. God, if that could be the case than she'd never park crooked at the grocery store ever again.

Jed West standing five feet away—ridiculous! Not improbable. Straight-up impossible. He was on her mind because of that silly coffee cup and her stressed-out brain manufactured a hallucination. Not altogether comforting, but then a psychotic break was preferable to encountering her ultimate sexual fantasy while sporting serious camel toe.

A short rapping knock came at the door. "Breezy?" Neve's peeved voice was a half step below testy.

She expelled a lungful of air, tightened her grip on her tote bag and stepped back into the hall. "Forgot to turn off the sink. Water conservation is very important." Her laugh came out thin and high.

Jed West wasn't a mirage. She was speaking to him, actual words out of her actual mouth. He made eye contact. Knew that she existed in this mad-spinning world. The downside was that he stared as if she'd sprouted a second head, one that insisted on belting out the Titanic theme song.

In Russian.

"Wait. You two are sisters?" Incredulity infused his syllables.

"Affirmative." Neve looped an arm around her waist. "Born eleven and a half months apart." And they were night and day. Neve defined dainty, at least on the surface. Although she was a former figure skater who'd followed in the footsteps of their mother, she held a black belt in Brazilian jujitsu. These days she took down dudes twice her body weight during weekly sparring sessions.

Breezy had a black belt too, hers just happened to be in bookworming. July had barely started and already she'd logged one hundred and sixty books on Goodreads, well on track to surpass her year-end goal of two hundred. Neve had inky hair, strong brows and a wide sulky mouth. Breezy was a placid dairy cow in comparison, big-eyed and big-boned. Not blonde enough to have more fun, nor sleekly brown enough to classify as an elegant brunette.

"I'm the big sister," Neve deadpanned the long-standing joke as the top of her head scrapped Breezy's shoulder.

Breezy licked her dry lips, fighting to remember how to put the English language into usable sentences. "So, um, Jed. What brings you here?" Yes. Good. A perfectly safe, *normal* question. Way better than "Mind if I step closer to better assess the nuances of your scent?"

"Heard you're in the market for a reader." His deep rumble was a chisel striking granite. The vibrations thrummed to her bones. "We stopped in the kid section to grab a book. Want to vet my choice?"

What she wanted to do was gather each of his words like a precious bloom, build a bouquet and hug it to her chest then skip through sun-dappled meadows. Her sister had pulled off the coup of the century–Dear, darling Neve, currently sporting a bemused *you're being a giant idiot* expression.

"Nah, as long as it's not *The Giving Tree* you'll be fine," Breezy said, fighting to regroup.

Neve huffed a husky "Oh good God" under her breath and the hall went into rapid decompression, all available oxygen whizzing through invisible cracks.

But she wasn't Neve of the quick comeback. Her tongue tied into a figure eight knot. "I . . . it's . . . the message . . . not good. Bad."

Great. Apparently she also took elocution lessons from Tarzan.

"I see." The bewilderment on his face begged to differ.

"Terrific little getting-to-know-you, Breezy, but Jed doesn't have all day and *you* need to get this show on the road." Neve stepped in, saving her from more self-inflicted humiliation.

The next twenty-five minutes passed in a blur. The crowd who'd braved the terrible weather had murmured with disappointment when Breezy stepped to the podium and announced that Coach Tor wasn't going to make the event after all. But the grumbles transformed into cries of delight as she announced the presence of Jed West. A mother in the back row praised, "Sweet Baby Jesus."

Breezy gave an internal nod in solidarity. *Amen, sister.*

After Jed announced his reading choice, his gaze skimmed the crowd before landing on her, in the back corner, arms locked to her chest to keep her heart from jumping out of her rib cage. Her stomach constricted. Talk about a visceral stare. It felt as intimate as a private caress. She could have sworn that he winked, but yeah . . . right.

Earth to Breezy, come in, please.

Guys who looked like Jed West didn't flirt with girls like her. By sixteen, her place in the social pecking order had been cemented. The friend. The funny one. The one packing junk in the trunk, who bought her own drinks at the club, and always got charged cover.

As if to confirm her theory, the moment vanished. He turned away, offering a view of his outrageously chiseled profile. The amount of scruff roughening the edge of his carved jaw was absolute perfection.

Opening the book, his rich velvety baritone imbued every cringe-worthy sentence with a sense of yearning and noble sacrifice. As he slowly flipped through the pages it was almost enough to convince her she'd been wrong to be such a hater.

"Guess this makes up for me forgetting your birthday for the past three years?" Neve leaned in beside her.

Breezy gave a giddy nod. "You get a pass for Christmas and birthdays forever more. Jed West is in my library. How did this happen?"

"What can I say?" Neve shrugged smugly. "Occupational perk."

"Of course, let the record show that I had no idea you were interviewing him today." Breezy leveled a bemused side eye. "That's a pretty big skeleton to hide in your closet."

"Way I saw it, I had two options if I fessed up." Her sister stared back without a shred of shame. "One, leave you green with envy or two, wonder if you'd turn up and stalk us from a back booth at Zachary's."

"You watched him eat?" She bounced on her toes and clapped her hands. "Details, details. Was it perfect?"

"There was chewing. Mouthed closed." Neve gave her chin a thoughtful rub. "Oh! He ordered orange juice. Fresh squeezed."

"Eeep!" Breezy swallowed herself, after a muffled moan. "You know I love juice."

"Guess you two are soul mates." Neve used only a pinch of her usual sarcasm, a small smile played on the edges of her mouth. "Honestly, I'm thrilled to have gotten to do this for you."

Wild applause broke out as Jed finished the last line of the book. It went on and on before eventually dwindling into an uncertain silence. Finally, he cleared his throat, seeking her out with a single raised brow. The implication was clear—what now?

"Oh! Right!" Breezy jolted from the wall, adrenaline flushing through her system. Time to host a short Q & A with the object of her most depraved lust while her butt cheeks chomped the skintight Lycra. "Let's take a few questions."

Every hand in the room shot toward the ceiling. Some kids waved both. Jed answered queries ranging from "What's your favorite number?" "Five," (same as his jersey), to "What's your favorite movie?" "*The Big Lebowski*," to his pregame rituals "Dressing left-to-right," and "Never shaving during playoffs."

When he absently combed his fingers through his hair, the faintest scent of freshly tilled earth crossed the podium. No wait, make that a cedar grove in snow. She sniffed deeply, catching base notes of Earl Grey, her favorite tea, before mentally shaking her head.

Stop! The head of the children's section wasn't allowed to get hot and bothered while promoting literacy. Or to sniff the special guests.

Neve made a subtle "wrap it up" gesture.

Breezy stepped close, tall enough she didn't have to whisper in his ear. A perk of being a five-foot-eleven giantess. "Ready to make a break for it? My sister will hustle you out."

He glanced over, covering the microphone and frowning slightly. "What about signing autographs?"

"Oh. I don't want to impose on your time." Impossible to tear her gaze from the way his lucky hand scrubbed his chin scruff, bristly brown hairs that looked as if they'd feel delicious dragged across bare skin.

"Wouldn't be right," he muttered to himself. "These are kids."

That's it. She was dead—an official ghost, one who'd roam the library as a happy phantom because she'd kicked the bucket in the best of ways, discovering her celebrity crush was an actual good guy, not just playing one on television.

The only improvement on the present moment would be if he happened to punch a fist to his sternum as if struck by a mortal blow. After a rueful head shake, he'd chuckle, a sound like a bag of gravel dragged through honey. "Breezy Angel," he'd murmur, as if her name was a Shakespearean sonnet. "Why . . . you're the one. The one that I've been waiting for my whole life."

"How do you want me?" he asked, speaking slow as if repeating himself.

A hectic heat fired up her neck. "Excuse me?"

He arched a brow. "Up against the wall?"

Her mouth opened but words formed a traffic jam in her one-lane throat.

"Jed! Take position by the exit!" Neve clapped her hands and strode toward the conference room double doors, in her element bossing people left and right. "Hey, listen up! Westy has graciously agreed to sign a few autographs on your way out. Form a line and keep it to one per person. Also, remember to stay dry and drive home safe. Thanks so much for coming out."

Her sister's brash voice served as a defibrillator, zapping Breezy back to life and the fact she was on the clock, not the steamy Playboy Grotto. "And . . ." She licked her too-dry lips before continuing, "Don't forget to sign up for the summer reading challenge by the checkout desk. Lots of great prizes to win, including tickets to the Hellions home opener next season. Unmask the Super Reader in you." Impulsively, she flexed her biceps in a double muscle pose.

The gesture tested the limits of the old costume.

Air-conditioned air kissed her suddenly bare skin as the threadbare material gave way in an audible rip. Make that her bare-ass skin.

Worse, she'd fallen behind on laundry and this morning the only clean underwear remaining in her dresser was her "Fox-trotting Foxes" thong.

Before the full impact of the fashion disaster could register, a crunch of Gore-Tex encircled her hips. A silent scream detonated deep inside her skull. Jed West had his actual hands on her actual body, albeit through his rain jacket that he pressed to her naked butt cheeks with enough force to staunch blood flow, or more aptly, her wounded pride.

The universe had a seriously sinister way of granting wishes. The pensive expression in his eyes couldn't be further from passionate ardor. This wasn't that sultry "Wanna play plant the parsnip?" look she'd imagined earlier. It was pity. She was an expert in being on the receiving end of those sorts of faces.

Tonight Jed would take some svelte *Sports Illustrated* model out for cocktails, tell her about his crazy day, and they'd laugh and laugh.

She'd be relegated to the punch line of a funny story, a walking, talking joke. Salt burned the insides of her eyelids, a warning that tears weren't lagging far behind.

"Why don't you borrow this and get changed?" Jed didn't sound as if he was fighting off a chuckle. No, he sounded grave, kind even.

Of course he did.

Everyone knew Westy was a good guy. The captain who always had complimentary words for the opposing team, never failed to yield the spotlight to teammates.

He'd offered to stick around and sign autographs for children, and now had been blinded by a jilted librarian's full moon. He wasn't going to mock her. But he wasn't going to really see her either, at least not as a woman. Just an awkward calamity.

"T-thank you." She stumbled, but he was already turning to walk toward Neve. As he reached for the first notepad pressed into his hand, a dozen camera phones flashed like paparazzi.

"Jed West?" Daisy, her librarian tech, sidled up with an incredulous laugh. "Wow! Way to throw a wrench into Tater Tots's plans. You might have bought us a reprieve today. No way can they shut us down after that stunt." Tater Tots was the secret code name for their dour boss, Janet Tater. The lady disliked anyone under the age of sixteen, and barely tolerated the boisterous noise that often floated from the children's department.

"Cover me," Breezy blurted, hoisting the jacket at her waist. "I have to go."

"What? Where?" Daisy's blond bob swung as she jerked back her head.

"I have a . . . uh a . . . to make an urgent call." Breezy scuttled backward, one hand clutching her exposed rump. The back exit led to the stairwell, one that would take her to the first floor. From there she could cut across the nonfiction section to the handicap bathroom and change. That toilet was rarely used so it was a safe place to release the tears building—hot and terrible— behind her twitching lids.

"You can't leave, I don't care if the pope is on the phone." Daisy flashed an incredulous look. "What's gotten into you? Jed West is here. *Your* Jed West."

In addition to the Westy mug, Breezy had a wall calendar of him hanging behind her desk, a gift from last year's office secret Santa. The library volunteers kept her supplied with a steady stream of fangirl-related gifs, memes and interview clips.

"Listen to me." Her self-control rapidly approached a breaking point. "I'm out of commission. *You* have to hold down the fort. Make sure these families don't leave without signing up for the summer reading challenge. Oh, and please thank my sister. She is amazing. A goddess."

Daisy stuck her hands on her hips, but before she could rattle off more questions Breezy barreled through the exit and into the stairwell. By the time she hit the main floor, she was panting.

"Breezy? Breezy, honey, what happened?" A concerned female voice piped from the reference desk. She didn't turn to see which of the senior volunteers asked the question. A couple of men waved from the public access computers as she blew past like a human tornado. At the last moment, she veered out the main exit.

The sliding doors opened and she burst into the parking lot, slamming a hand shield over her eyes to peer through the downpour.

Screw the bathroom. Better to get the hell out of Dodge and fast.

The trouble was that her purse was locked in her bottom desk drawer. Ah, wait. She sighed in relief. A spare key was hidden behind the bumper. Squatting, she fished it out as the costume's fabric ripped more. Her hamstrings were now exposed too, but whatever, the worst of damage was done. Opening the door to her yellow Volkswagen Beetle, she climbed into the driver's seat.

Rain hammered the roof like a furious punctuation to the whole sorry affair. "Oh my God," she muttered between ragged breaths. But that didn't come close to releasing the hot emotion building inside her, squeezing each rib like a vise.

"Fuck!" She punched the steering wheel like a boxer's speed ball. "Fuck. Fuck. Fuckity Fuck Fuckolahhh-hhhhh . . . *ouch*!" Her knuckles exploded in pain as the horn gave way with a wheezily annoyed toot.

Shoving the key in the ignition, she eased out of the parking lot, heading toward home.

Home. *Her* home. The ink hadn't even dried on her mortgage, purchased last month as an act of independence, a sign that she could make it on her own without the support of a crappy fiancé.

Neighborhoods passed by in a blur, same with the pedestrians taking shelter under umbrellas. With her foot pressed to the accelerator, it was tempting to steer out of the city. Drive straight out of Denver, through the foothills and into the Rockies masked behind the roiling clouds. Surely a nice log cabin waited in the woods.

An out-of-the-way place where she could whittle a staff from a thick branch and use it to scare away trespassers.

Except that plan would never work. She loved her bed. It was the one place that accepted her just the way she was, day or night, rain or shine. A safe refuge to binge on *Parks and Recreation* while wallowing in self-pity and Pepperidge Farm cookie crumbs.

She turned onto her street.

God Saw You Do That read this week's sign out in front of Trinity Church. The pastor changed the marquee every Wednesday.

"Big deal," she snarled, gripping the wheel. "So did Jed West." A conga line of horrific memories paraded through her head. Namely Westy getting an eyeful of her fox-printed thong and extra fifteen pounds.

It wasn't until she slammed into the garage and flung open the driver's side door that she registered what was still tied around her waist. She fingered the Gore-Tex with a groan.

Talk about taking a shitty situation and drizzling a dollop of sucks-to-be-you over the top. It wasn't enough to flash Jed her wobbly bits, she had to go and steal his rain jacket too. And if on the million—no, scratch that, billion to one—chance that the sexy look he'd given her up on the podium wasn't a figure of her imagination, well she'd blown it now.

Face meet palm.

Chapter Four

"HOUSTON, WE HAVE a problem." Neve poked Jed in the ribs with a remarkably pointy elbow. "My sister stole your jacket."

"Nah, it's fine. I loaned it to her." Jed finished signing his last autograph and waved goodbye to the curly haired kid and his dad, buoyed by the relief that his vision hadn't gone awry since leaving Zachary's. No nagging headache. No dizziness. Maybe the blurriness was nothing but a blip. "I'll swing by her desk and grab it on the way out."

He wouldn't mind getting one last peek at the voluptuous librarian with the classic pinup features. Those traffic-stopping curves had been replaying in the back of his mind for the past half hour. As an unabashed ass man, he couldn't help but notice that Breezy Angel sported a damn near perfect apple butt. He'd almost gotten wood from the tear in her suit, except the peep show had been unintended and the shame in her eyes overrode his lust.

"Yeah, about that. No. You won't." Neve appeared irritated. "She drove home. I just got her text."

"She's gone?" He patted his sweats. *Shit.* No pockets. No wallet. His plan was to spend the afternoon lifting at the gym, not hanging at a library. When he'd parked, he'd pulled it out from his gym bag and stuck it inside his jacket pocket. Now it had gone off to a stranger's house who lived who the hell knows where.

"You need to understand. My sister, she was . . ." Neve turned up her palms, dismay radiating from every feature. "Flustered."

Not the word he'd have gone with but *luscious* sure as hell wouldn't fly in the current situation. "I need her address." At least he'd secured his Land Rover key into the clip in his waistband, an old habit from when he'd trail run in the redwoods north of San Francisco Bay.

Neve stiffened at his request, but her shoulders relaxed after his explanation about how it would be easier to retrieve the jacket and wallet himself. "It's only a couple of minutes out of my way." He talked fast, as if verbal speed could mask his edginess. A slight frown creased his brow. He wasn't the type to get the fucking jitters. His even-keeled temperament was a source of pride. Mental toughness wasn't just for the rink, but the bedrock upon which he built the foundation of his life.

But fifteen minutes later, as he pulled his Land Rover up in front of the address he'd plugged into the GPS, his pulse accelerated to fifth gear.

"You have arrived at your destination," the navigation voice intoned.

He peered through his rain-drenched windshield. Breezy Angel's house barely qualified as a cottage, with white shutters and shingles painted a robin's egg blue. Despite the shitty weather, the tiny place radiated a cheerful glow. Buttery light poured from the two front windows that were framed by cheerful sunflowers.

After setting the handbrake, he caught sight of his goofy half smile in the rearview mirror. He looked like a goddamn giddy teenager going to prom or some shit. Time to slow his roll. All he was here to do was grab his coat and go.

"Grab and go," he repeated, slamming the door. "Grab and go."

He dashed from the car to the front porch, but received no answer to his knock. Bluesy music played inside, overlaid by the sounds of muffled swearing. Someone was home at least. He knocked again, using more force. A creak of footsteps drew near followed by the unsettling sense of being scrutinized through the peep hole. He waved.

More muffled swearing. He chewed at the corner of his top lip, eyebrows raised. This sweet-faced children's librarian knew curses that could shame a locker room of disgruntled hockey players.

"Uh, hello?" He leaned closer. "Breezy? Everything okay?"

Two summers ago, he'd taken a trip to South Africa, went cage-diving with great whites. The tour operator had chummed the water and the sea turned red with bloody fish guts. It hadn't taken long for the great beasts to emerge from the deep gloom and attack the cage in a mindless frenzy. The sounds emitting from inside the cottage were almost as wild. Furniture getting dragged. A distant door slammed again and again.

What the hell was she doing in there, hiding bodies?

After a long minute, he raised his hand to knock for a third time, but this time the door swung open as if on cue. His throat throbbed like he'd been cross-checked in the trachea.

No sign of the destroyed costume. Instead the librarian had replaced her ruined superhero suit with a tight T-shirt that read I Still Believe in 398.2, a cardigan and black skull and crossbones leggings that accentuated her heart-pounding waist-to-hip ratio. All that thick, glossy hair was tied up with a red polka-dot scarf like that vintage World War II mascot. Don't forget the thick black-framed glasses. The whole effect was classic housewife meets naughty nerd, and it worked like a fucking treat.

Blood rerouted to his cock. Oh yeah, he liked this.

He liked it a lot.

"You." The tip of her pink tongue darted out, flicking across the small indentation in her top lip. "You're here."

"Yeah." He glanced down to his rain-splattered sneakers and back to her stunned face. "Looks like I am."

A long silence ensued. As he stood there, an unexpected feeling of rightness settled over him as if standing on Breezy Angel's porch wasn't the culmination of a series of unfortunate events, but part of a grand and mysterious plan.

He chuckled, but the sound was hollow in his ears—his dumb ass better wise up real fast. He wasn't some regular Joe Blow swinging by to grab a missing jacket from a pretty girl. He was Jed West, Hellions captain.

Wasn't that all people ever saw?

The name.

The fame.

Not that celebrity went to his head all that much—a thousand fans cheering could go to a thousand fans booing in a single play. On shitty nights, that's exactly what happened.

But he didn't need to dash off invitations to a pity party. After all, he made a great living playing an even greater game. The lack of privacy, the critics, the curious fans and even the recent self-chosen celibacy went part and parcel with the territory. If he wanted to play, he had to pay the piper somewhere.

He jerked his head toward where the rain was doing its level best to erode the sidewalk. "I loaned you my Gore-Tex and—"

"Sorry, yes. Oh God. You're right. I'm sorry." She stared, horrified. "What an idiot. Me, I mean. *I'm* the idiot. Not you. You are definitely not an idiot."

Amusement tugged at the corner of his mouth, his lips slowly spreading into another wide smile. She was funny.

He liked it.

He liked her.

"I normally keep my wallet in my back pocket but . . ." He made a vague gesture toward his sweatpants-clad ass, privately cursing his own awkwardness. "No pockets," he concluded lamely.

"Of course. And come in, please. It's so wet." Her brows wrinkled in panic. "I'm totally making you stand there. Sorry. Sorry."

Her gorgeous round, silver-blue eyes were nearly at his level. Damn she was tall. "You know something? You apologize a lot," he observed wryly.

"Bad habit. Sorry." She smashed her lips, wincing. "See? I finally quit biting my nails, but making random apologies? Forget about it. I'll be on my deathbed asking for forgiveness from the nurses."

She backed away and he stepped over the threshold. The yellow-walled interior smelled like fresh paint. "Nice place." And it was. Warm and cozy. A lot like its owner.

"I thought so too, until I got home today." She plucked his jacket from the back of her love seat. "Now it's being a jerk. My stupid roof has sprung a leak."

The living room was lined with cardboard boxes, as if she'd recently moved in. Framed museum posters were stacked in the corner. The only things set up in here were her four bookshelves. "Can I be of any help?"

"How?" Her lips parted in apparent surprise. "You do home repairs?"

He shrugged, a knot loosening the too-tight muscles between his shoulders. "Once upon a time I worked summers as a handyman for a Sunnyvale contractor, an old football buddy of my brother's. Let's see the problem."

"Um . . . well." She fiddled with a string dangling off the wrist of her cardigan, and broke it with a sharp twist. "It's in my bedroom."

The silence lasted several awkward beats before a deep-set dimple made an appearance in her left cheek. He swallowed back an impulse to lick it. Was she fucking with him?

She must have noticed his hesitation because she made the sign of the cross over her heart. "Promise this isn't a set up for a cheesy seventies porno. You might want to stick on that raincoat though. Fair warning."

While he laughed, her gaze darted from his head to his toes, a quick appraisal, but an appraisal nevertheless. He didn't quite know how to read her. Her demeanor wasn't forwardly flirtatious, but that pink in her cheeks hinted that she didn't mind what she saw.

And the feeling was mutual, more than mutual if the sudden snugness in his boxer briefs was any indication.

He tried and failed not to gawk at her ass as she

walked ahead of him down a narrow hallway. It had been a long time since he'd held a soft woman.

When Breezy turned, they stood almost chest to chest, and her eyes. Fucking fuck. Those eyes were something else.

"Um." She cleared her throat. "Here we are."

Her bedroom.

He hoped his gaze stayed neutral, vaguely helpful, rather than reveal the dirty fantasies that swirled through his brain like an X-rated kaleidoscope.

Christ. His boxers were fitting snugger still, if he kept going like this he'd be tenting his sweats. He flexed his legs and wildly tried to focus on something—anything—that wasn't Breezy on her knees, working that lush mouth over his cock, or having those two perfect-ten tits bouncing in his hands as she rode him reverse cowgirl.

Look, he wasn't a pervert, but fuck it, he was a man . . . and a creative lover in the right moment.

Which this sure as hell wasn't.

Paper cut to the eyeball. No, wait paper cuts to the dick. Yeah, a legal document right on the tip.

That ball-shrinking thought worked its necessary magic.

Without another word, she opened the door and the trouble was immediately obvious. A wet ring of plaster formed in the ceiling as a steady drizzle *drip, drip, dripped* into a metal mixing bowl placed in the center of an antique brass bed.

"Total disaster, right?" Worry etched her words. "I closed on this place two weeks ago, and all my savings are sunk into the down payment. The home inspector made it sound like the roof had another five years of life. If it needs replacing then I can't even afford tears."

He pushed up his sweatshirt sleeves. Fantasies would have to wait. The damage wasn't good, but there was no way of knowing what the problem's extent was until he examined the source of the leak. "I'm going to need to access the attic. Where's your crawl space?"

"There's a trap door to the ceiling in the closet." Small lines bracketed her pressed mouth. "I haven't braved exploring up there yet, on account of spiders and—"

"Don't worry. I'm on it." He dropped his coat onto the foot of the bed and strode toward her bedroom's closet.

"No! Stop." She dive-bombed in front of the door, splaying out her arms as if to ward him off. "Not there. In the hallway!"

He froze, studying her face for a long second. Rain drummed hard on the roof, the noise growing in intensity. What was she hiding? Piles of dirty laundry? Her bras and underwear?

Her body jolted as if she was trying to suppress a shiver. The notion bored into his stomach, hot and hungry. Was she feeling it too, the same tightening in the chest as if robbed of air, this attraction, like a tether, pulling them together?

He glanced down, fighting to get a grip. After all,

what culled the boys from the men was self-control. "I need a bucket, a flashlight, caulking and a tarp."

She toyed with one of her earrings, absorbing his request. The wind picked up, branches from the cherry tree outside her window scratching at the glass. "My stepdad set up a utility area in the garage. A little ambitious of him when I can't tell apart a Phillips and flathead screwdriver . . ." She broke off, as the water dripping from the ceiling gushed into an indoor waterfall.

She groaned, as chunks of plaster fell onto her bed. "I'm so freaking screwed."

Her wide gaze was panicked, *shit*, those might even be tears. "No." Before he could weigh the consequences of his action, he took hold of her upper arms, holding tight. "You're going to be okay, understand?" It wasn't until he spoke that he realized how fucking intense he sounded, like this was the finale in a war movie, and he was asking her to do battle by his side.

But she didn't laugh. Hell, she didn't even crack a smile as he released her, taking two steps back. Just gave a dazed nod, idly massaging the spot near her shoulder where his palm had touched.

"Back in a second," he muttered, heading to her garage to rummage for the necessary tools. As he poked around the workbench, he caught himself whistling under his breath. Whistling "Eye of the Tiger" to be exact.

He gaped at the wood pegboard in front of him. Since walking into Breezy's library, there'd been no sign of the unsettled question that had been nagging him with a near-constant tenacity since the playoffs, the one that twisted his gut in the middle of the night, woke him from a dead sleep, chest sheened in sweat, hands flung in front of his face as if bracing for impact.

Who would he be without hockey? If he quit the game.

For now, an afternoon, he seemed to be granted a reprieve. Instead, he could pretend to be an ordinary guy who helped a pretty woman fix her leaky roof, a nice, simple—ordinary—distraction from his greater problems.

He returned to the hallway and the pretty lady in question waited by the open closet door. He gave her a reassuring smile, ducked inside and lowered the attic ladder.

"Careful," she called anxiously. "Don't drown up there."

"One question." He climbed up a few rungs and paused, glancing back over one shoulder. "In case anything should happen."

Her eyes widened. "Okay?"

"I'm dying to know." He pointed at the front of her shirt and arched a brow. "What's a 398.2?"

"Huh?" She peered down at her chest, and the phrase I Believe in 398.2. emblazoned across her chest. "Oh. Hah. A little Dewey decimal librarian humor. That's the area where we shelve fairy tales."

"I believe in fairy tales," he mused. Something in

her dreamy eyes kept him rooted to the spot. "So what, you're an old-fashioned romantic, eh?"

"I guess." She toyed with a stray lock of hair, twisting it absently. "But so far I've only kissed frogs. No princes."

"Well, I'll do my best to be your knight in shining armor," he joked, hoisting himself into her attic. Inching along, he followed the wet rafter line to the source of the leak, one big enough to require tar.

She gripped the closet door as he remerged. "How bad is it?" Her words came out tight. "Don't sugarcoat. Shoot straight. I can take it."

"You need a handyman more than a knight. A temporary patch will stop the bleeding and last through the storm. Is there a hardware store in the neighborhood?"

She thought a moment. "Norman Tool Supplies is a few blocks away. But you've already gone above and beyond and this isn't your problem. I can take it from here."

Her confident tone belied her panicked expression.

He took another step closer and inhaled the scent in her shampoo. Sweet, but sexy, no cloying perfumes, just a hint of coconut. An image flashed in his mind. Her, oiled up on a Hawaiian beach with a colorful sarong slung around her hips, draping her curvy waist. The idea caused a low hum in his gut, like a key turning in an ignition. "I'll be back in fifteen," he muttered, turning for the door, his pace quick.

For all he overthought his game, his training regime,

his whole damn life, for once he didn't want to ponder his current behavior too hard. This afternoon was venturing beyond the scope of a simple Good Samaritan. But like the state of his head, maybe it was better not to know what the hell was going on.

Chapter Five

BREEZY REPLACED THE rapidly filling bucket on her bed with an empty one, trying not to stress over the fact that a sizeable section of her ceiling had crumbled over her pretty pale blue comforter. She headed for her laundry room to dump out the water in the utility sink. If Charles Dickens could be resurrected for the thankless task of penning Breezy's biography, today's chapter would no doubt begin with: It was the best of times, it was the worst of times.

Jed West was in her home. Repeat: Jed. West. Was. In. Her. Home.

And not just in her house, but up her attic, and that wasn't a "wink nudge" euphemism. He'd driven to the neighborhood hardware store and returned with a plastic bag bulging with supplies that suggested, true to his word, he knew exactly what he was doing.

And while she didn't want to get greedy with miracles, if the universe could allow him to halt the deluge soaking through the roof and save her room from becoming the newest city wetland, the gesture would be mightily appreciated.

That and not have him discover that hidden in her bedroom closet was a horde of Jed West memorabilia. When she'd seen him hunched on the porch through her peephole, her brain had flatlined. She'd sprung into frantic action, whirling through the house, grabbing all her fangirl items. First and foremost, the life-size cardboard cutout of him that her bestie, Margot, had nabbed from a downtown sports bar last month. The poster graced her bedroom door like a teenybop celebrity. The fridge magnets. The mug. The bobblehead plastic toy on the sink windowsill.

"All good." He emerged from the attic door feet first, gripping the ceiling and lowering himself down in one steady, controlled motion, suggestive of years spent working out on pull-up bars. His sweatshirt rode high over his belly button, revealing a slab of lean, hard-cut abdominal muscles. A warrior's body, with one thick silvery scar running parallel across his hip, alongside a thick, delicious-looking vein that disappeared into his elastic waistband.

It was overwhelming, enduring this much physical longing.

"That patch should hold for the rest of the storm," he spoke with no clue that she was on the verge of melting into a pool of lust. "I slapped on two coats of tar."

"I can't thank you enough." She forced her gaze up as he casually tugged down his hoodie, staring past her with a frown.

"Shit. Your bed is soaked."

It took a moment for anything but the last word to register. She ground her knees together, acutely aware of the damp slickness in her own panties. *That ain't the only thing wet around here.*

Jesus, she could host her own creepy standup routine on Comedy Central. Her pink-cheeked reflection beamed back from the full-length mirror on the wall, her eyes were glazed with visible arousal. This was so uncool. And typical Breezy behavior.

On her tombstone it would read: *She came. She saw. She made it awkward.*

"You should strip off the sheets and position the mattress over the heating vent," he continued, just as the front door banged with a short sharp rap.

"That must be Neve," she said, flustered. "She can help me flip it off the baseboards. I'll take the comforter down to the cleaners to see what they can do. So anyway, thanks. You've done so much today. Above and beyond."

What're you thinking, crazy? Hurrying Jed West out of here? Her subconscious screeched in Margot's voice, urging her to throw her body in front of the door. Offer to tap dance. Or lap dance. Or a cup of coffee. Or hell, a blow job.

But her best friend was off doing downward dogs in

Baja and no use in the advice department until she returned at summer's end.

Breezy had no choice but to push the protesting howl aside. Jed West might have spoken at her library and patched her leaky roof, but he was also a hockey god. Surely he had better things to do. Return to Mount Olympus and melt the snowcap with his superhuman hotness. Or enjoy a threesome with nubile goddesses. Or do whatever it is that gods do when not slumming with mere mortals.

"I'm serious. You're doing me the favor. Look, that rain's coming down harder by the minute."

For a god, he seemed in no hurry to escape back to his exalted realm. And he did have a point. The eaves were overflowing outside the corner window with Niagara-like force.

"Honestly it was no big deal. I like odd jobs." His encouraging smile gave her enough lift to float to the front door. It was almost like he enjoyed being in her orbit, that he was . . . interested.

Which was crazy.

Crazier than crazy.

Almost as crazy that at some point during the past thirty minutes, Jed had begun morphing from some abstract celebrity fantasy to an actual flesh and blood man. A guy who did fix-it jobs and made her laugh even as she drooled over the sinewy muscles in his forearms.

The growing heat between her legs pulsed.

But it wasn't until she'd turned the front doorknob

and stared at her mom and Granny Dee huddled under an umbrella stamped with the red pitchfork, the Hellions logo, that it felt like she was in danger of losing her mind.

"Shit!" She slapped a hand over her mouth and braced the doorframe to steady herself. Her legs had gone wobbly, as if the bones evaporated.

Mom sized up her leggings with a dismayed frown. They had an ongoing disagreement on whether or not they were pants. As per usual, Mom's makeup and outfit were perfect and she looked impossibly beautiful. It wasn't uncommon for strangers to mistake her for Diane Lane when out in public. "Guess that's one way to greet guests."

"S-sorry," she stammered as they barreled into her living room. Her stomach tumbled in a sickening lurch because right now, right this very second, Jed West was dismantling her bed.

And in the bewildered excitement of his proximity, she'd spaced out about the sex toys stowed under the mattress.

The magic wand.

The rabbit.

The weird-shaped purple one that oscillated.

The personal lubricant.

Despite Mom's disapproval, *shit* didn't come close to conveying the horror circulating through her bloodstream, turning her veins to acid. This was a screwup of epic proportions, even for her.

"What's the matter, Bumper Butt?" Granny Dee briskly untied her plastic rain bonnet, finger combing her fire-engine red curls back into place. "Sorry to waltz in unannounced, but you know how much I wanted a peek at your new place." She turned ninety in a few weeks, but moved like a woman in her sixties, as she bustled around the room, making approving noises over the curtain choices and knick-knacks on display.

Breezy ground two fists into her eyes with enough force to see stars. *Think. Think.* Two of the biggest hockey fanatics in the Denver metro area were pacing the room's perimeter while fifteen feet away a certifiable Hottie McHotterson was in her bedroom discovering her secret trove of sex toys.

And to think she'd actually believed the day's low point was ripping the ass out of her superhero suit.

What were her current options? Fake a seizure?

No. She gave her head an inward shake. Too dramatic. Plus, the last thing she needed to compound this situation were paramedics and a fire truck. A fake faint would be better. She could blame the episode on dehydration. Mom was always nagging her to drink more.

But in the end, she was too freaked out to manage anything other than the awful truth. At least the PG version.

She waved them close. "Jed West is here." She moved her lips like a ventriloquist, trying to keep her voice modulated as low as possible.

"What's that?" Her mom ignored her gesture, peering at the windows. She moved in short, graceful bursts with the energy of a hummingbird. Breezy always felt like a lumbering walrus in comparison.

"Oh, honey," Mom made a tut-tut sound. "Look at this grime. Didn't you promise that you were going to clean the tracks the last time I was here? How many times do I have to tell you that it only takes a sprinkle of baking soda and vinegar. Let it sit for five minutes and the gunk will wipe right off—"

"Enough with the tracks. Huddle up and listen." Screw her mom's anal clean freak obsessions. "Jed West is here," she breathed.

"Huh?" Granny Dee stuck a hand behind her ear. "God hates a mumbler."

A hard thud emanated from the bedroom. No doubt the queen-size mattress getting turned on its side. Stars danced on the edge of her vision.

Mom's eyes widened behind her tortoiseshell frames as she blew back her bangs. "Who's back there?"

"I'm worried about her coloring." Granny Dee pinched Breezy's cheeks. "It's this lousy weather. Where do you keep the whiskey? A nice hot toddy will warm you up."

Breezy strained her ears but silence reigned from the bedroom. At least Jed hadn't bolted out of the room, arms windmilling in horror at her sexual depravity. Maybe they'd be adults about this. After all, masturbating was a normal part of life, a common to-do item on the ol' weekly routine.

Shave legs.

Moisturize.

Use sunscreen.

Buy milk and eggs.

Get rocks off.

Studies showed it was better than melatonin for sleep.

But still . . . that didn't mean she wanted to discuss her vibrator preferences or lube choices with the actual embodiment of these dirty fantasies.

Panic simmered in her stomach. This was all so awful that it couldn't be happening.

Bump. Another hard thud. Followed by the *snickity-snick* roll of something plastic across the hardwood.

"There. I hear it again!" Mom clutched her purse to her chest, eyes wide. "Someone is in your bedroom."

Her mother had a gift for stating the obvious.

"Is it a man?" Granny Dee rubbed her hands with undisguised glee.

"Of course not!" Mom gave a disparaging shake of the head. "This is Breezy, not Margot."

She didn't mean those words as an insult. Still, Breezy flinched. She wasn't a play-the-field girl like her bestie who had a different guy lined up for a date every single Saturday night. From the look of her friend's Instagram account, her time in Mexico consisted of doing a lot of sun salutations and a lot, a lot, of very muscled surfers.

Breezy had never played the field. Her only serious

boyfriend had been Rory and he'd strung her along for years. Whenever she pushed to set an official date for the wedding, he'd mumble that his job pressures were too high. That he couldn't be the provider he wanted to be. A change of subject always came fast and furious. Whenever she had a problem at work, he'd dismiss it, but if he had an issue then stop the presses, this was a public emergency, ladies and gentlemen. He'd text her all day, no matter what was going on or how busy her schedule.

She made room. Accommodated. Because isn't that what people do in functional adult relationships?

Except two people had to do the giving. In Rory's case, she'd given and given and given until . . .

God. Any wonder that she despised *The Giving Tree*?

Once Rory's career was poised to take off with his long-anticipated promotion, she booked a dinner at a fancy bistro to toast the tomorrows that could finally become today. Instead, he had broken the news over the second glass of merlot. The promotion was tied to a move to the Boston office. She had just started to wrap her head around what it meant to leave her family and summon enthusiasm for New England, when he dropped the second bomb.

The one where she wasn't included in the relocation package.

His words exploded over her like lobbed grenades.

I need to buckle down and have space. Put me first for once. Focus on my career.

Blah. Blah. Fuck you. As if she'd ever taken up space in his world.

But to pour salt in the stinging wound, once he moved, Rory had met someone. Another lawyer. They went on a skiing vacation. Traveled to Iceland. Posed in the fall colors and hammed it up in a witch shop in Salem.

For a while, she'd stalked his Facebook account like a midnight masochist. She wasn't proud. But he'd dated this chick for six months before posting news of the elopement. They'd driven to New York City and gotten married in spring in Central Park, posing for selfies afterward on top of the Empire State Building.

Turned out Rory wasn't dragging his feet on marriage. Just marriage to *her*. Breezy had been the safe backup choice, as comforting as a well-worn pair of UGG boots.

Ugh was right.

"I know! Honey, focus!" Mom seized her shoulders and shook. "Where's that pepper spray that I bought you last Christmas?"

"Stop." She twisted free of her mother's grip. "There isn't a burglar. I had a problem with the roof. It leaked. It's getting fixed."

"All this excitement makes me want to pee." Granny Dee shuffled toward the bathroom. "And to sneak peek at your handyman."

When her grandma's screech followed a few seconds later, Breezy squeezed her eyes shut. Granny Dee had found Jed West. The only hope was that he wasn't double fisting two lipstick vibrators.

They'd been on sale, two for one, which seemed like a deal at the time.

Granny lurched back into the room, eyes the size of tea saucers. "There is . . . there is . . . there is . . ."

"Sit down. I said *sit*. I've got your blood pressure meds right here in your pocketbook."

Jed West appeared hot on Granny's heels and the sight took Breezy's breath.

How did he go through life looking like that? Did he ever get stuck ogling his reflection, transfixed by that face, those eyes, that chin. A modern day Narcissus?

Of course not.

He seemed comfortable and casual in his own skin. It must be like living in Paris or Venice, someplace where tourists showed up and fired off five hundred thousand photos and *oohed* and *ahhed* while locals went about their daily business.

"Hope I didn't frighten you," he said to Granny Dee in his deep voice.

Mom screamed. Not one of those Beatles fan crying and jumping up and down moments. More like opening a closet door only to discover ET nestled among the clothes requesting to phone home.

"Granny, sit in the rocking chair. I'm going to fetch you a glass of water. Mom. Take the love seat," she ordered with a confidence that she in no way felt.

But someone had to take charge and it wouldn't

do to add two heart attacks to the cluster. She quickly filled Mom and Granny in on the bare details of what had happened, Neve bringing Jed to the library as a surprise special guest. The jacket theft (minus the accidental mooning). The roof leaking. Turning, she found his gaze on her. "Jed?" It still sounded so weird to speak his name.

"Yeah?" He answered like it was normal.

Because it is his name, Stupid.

She blinked twice. "Mind helping me in the kitchen?"

While he might be a god, he was also slumming it among mortals and her family looked ready to stroke out. It was all hands on deck.

"Sure." He followed her into the tiny galley kitchen. When searching for a home to buy, she had craved an open plan living and kitchen area, but right now was grateful for the ability to shut the door. She leaned against it and pressed her hands to her cheeks. "Okay. Brace yourself. Some of my family members happen to be pretty big Hellions fans."

Some being code for every single woman in her bloodline.

He digested the information. "And you?" He asked the question casually, but it had a loaded feeling.

She shrugged, feigning nonchalance to hide her agitation. Outright lying was always a bad idea, but this didn't seem the time to mention she had a cardboard cutout of his likeness in her closet.

Was there ever really a good time to share such information?

"I . . . you know . . ." She cleared her throat. "Hockey is a good game. Exciting, I guess. If you're into that sort of thing." Uh, which she was. In fact, she had a family rep for hurling handfuls of cheese and caramel popcorn at the screen during bad calls.

"But you're not a fan?" Obvious relief lit his eyes. "That's good. Real good."

"It is?" She wanted to press him, ask follow-up questions, namely "why?" but the only part of her cognitive functioning that seemed operational was the area that controlled basic vital functions. And from the freaked-out way her breath hitched and her heart pounded, even that was pushing her physiological luck.

"Breezy? Honey? Join us a moment?" Her mother's voice rang out from the living room. It had a stilting, formal, polite quality. As if they were strangers. "In your room if you please."

She needed a fire engine hose to put out the burn in her cheeks. "Crap, my room, moving the bed . . . you saw. . . ." She couldn't even say the words.

Sex. Toys.

My sex toys.

Oh God. Oh God. Oh God.

Now it was his turn to blush and the unexpected sight nearly catapulted her heart from her chest. "I moved your, uh, special things into the laundry basket."

"Special things?" Her voice squeaked. "That's one way of putting it." Jed West had touched her vibrators. It could almost be sexy if it wasn't absolutely horrifying.

A box of red wine perched on the third shelf in her pantry. She could barricade herself inside and position her mouth directly under the spigot. While it might not be possible to drink the shame away, she was willing to give it her best shot.

"Your grandma burst in and I had to think fast. Didn't want to give her a stroke. Haven't taken a CPR class in a while." That smile might be "boy next door" but those eyes were straight-up bad boy. Right now, he didn't resemble the most respected and beloved hockey player in the state. Just a good-looking guy with dirty thoughts on the brain. "Quite the collection you have."

And in this weird alternate universe of her kitchen, she wasn't a dumpy librarian who couldn't keep even a subpar man, but the object of desire.

"Seemed more fun than stamps or spoons." She subtly pinched the soft flesh of her inner elbow. Hard. Trying to find her center again. "Anyway. Looks like you . . . uh . . . you . . . rescued me again." And while saving her from sex toy shaming wasn't exactly a moment to be memorialized in the next Disney movie, no white knight could have done better.

His wicked smile heated her to the tips of her toes. She'd seen his grin a thousand times on television, and on occasion had even wondered what it would feel like to be on the receiving end of such perfection. Turned out that the answer was so good that her mind had never had a chance in trying to comprehend.

"Breezy!" This time there was a definite squawk to Mom's voice.

Ah, memories. That was the same tone Mom had used when Breezy klutzed through yet another one of her figure skating classes. Never a good look when the coach's daughter was unable to make it through a session without turning her butt black and blue.

This afternoon might have been an opportunity to slip into a wonderful alternate universe, but everyday reality was right there, down the hall.

"Hold that thought," she burst out.

"How do you know what I'm thinking?" His eyes were something else, bits of green and gold, with a smoldering expression that threatened to leave her panties in cinders.

She blinked, fighting for equilibrium. "I am sure it's all sugar and spice. After all, you were an altar boy for how long again?"

"Eight years." His smile wilted. "How do you know that?"

She slammed her lips shut, teetering on the edge of the conversational cliff. What was going to be next? *I happen to know pretty much everything about you, Westy. Thanks to my mindless midnight stalking sessions on the internet, I've built up quite the dossier. Birthdate: April 29th. Sign: Taurus. Hometown: Sausalito, California. Sibling: One, brother. Father: Living. Retired transplant surgeon from UCSF. Mother: Living. Homemaker. Favorite food: Burgers. Wife: None.*

How about hell and no.

Jed couldn't know that. He'd think she was crazy pants.

"Breezy Jane Angel!" Using the middle name. Mom was dragging out the big guns.

"Here's the deal." Breezy took a deep breath. Better to avoid a bald-faced lie in favor of a delicate dance of omission. "My mom and grandma are *yuuuge* hockey fans. My big sister is a sports journalist. I catch lots of random gossip on players." All true. In the way that she could also say "last night I ate chicken for dinner" . . . double cheese chicken BBQ pizza. A whole medium. Alone. In underwear while watching *Girls* on HBO.

Details, shmeee-tails.

She ducked out of the kitchen before he could respond. All her fun fangirling felt a whole lot less creepier before meeting him, before seeing him as an actual person and not a scruffy masculine jaw and chiseled six-pack.

"Look at my arms?" Her mother hiked up her sleeves as she slipped into her room. "I've got chills."

"Not me. I'm hot, hot, hot." Granny Dee did a hip shimmy that was so wrong that it made the full three-sixty turn back to right.

"Shoo! Go home, you two!" Breezy waved toward the front door. "And call Neve. She'll explain how this all came to pass. I'll fill in the rest. Later."

Mom took a few halting steps in the direction of the front door, but Granny Dee hurtled the coffee table and tore off for the kitchen. Guess those fish oil tablets she swallowed with her morning orange juice paid off. While her fitness was impressive, it would be nice if it wasn't used to do gossipy reconnaissance.

By the time Breezy caught up, Granny had a ball-point pen out and was rummaging through her purple leather handbag. "All I have in here is my dang check-book," she muttered. "It'll have to do. I'm not leaving until I get an autograph. The ladies in my water aerobics class are going to pee the pool when I tell them how I met Jed West."

"Sorry," Breezy mouthed over the top of her head.

Jed signed a stub and passed it over. "You're my number one fan?" he teased.

"I like you fine, boy, but Patchy has my heart." Granny had a thing for Patrick "Patch" Donnelly, the ginger-bearded goalie, probably because he was a former seminarian, a good Catholic boy. "Anyway your number one fan is—"

"I think this has been enough excitement for one afternoon." Breezy grabbed her grandmother by the elbow and steered her out the kitchen, propelling them toward the front door. "I'll see you both at the picnic." The Angel Fourth of July party was in three days and a firm family tradition. "Now get home safe before the streets flood. And before you ask, Mom, no I haven't bought the flag cake ingredients, but never fear, I'll bring it." Her specialty, she made the dessert for the party every year.

Granny Dee's look indicated she wasn't fooled, not even a little. Still, she allowed herself to be ushered out onto the covered porch. "You bringing a date to the picnic? Seeing as you are a single and all." She spoke the second sentence loudly from out of the corner of her twisted mouth.

Breezy cringed. This was a habit among the women in her family. They said anything they pleased under the mistaken belief that if it happened to be uttered from the corner of their mouth, no one would ever be the wiser.

The problem was . . . everyone with functional eardrums heard too, even road construction crews jackhammering out on I-70.

"Why not invite Jed?" Granny stage-whispered. "See if he can bring a friend." She waggled her thin drawn-in brows. "Maybe the Hellion defensive line."

"No way." Breezy shook her head. "Why would he ever want to come to that?"

Mom appeared to think it over. "Mention Neve will attend if she doesn't have to do the work trip."

Resentment sluiced through Breezy's stomach, a familiar gnawing envy that burned her insides. "What's that mean?"

"Look how he came to your library at your sister's request. I bet he likes her." She glanced at Granny with visions of rink side season passes dancing before her eyes. "Imagine that. Jed and Neve."

Jed and Neve?

Jed and Neve!

Over Breezy's dead body.

She swallowed back the "What am I? Chopped liver?" retort.

No point.

In Mom's eyes, Neve had always come first. Not only by birthright but also affection. It wasn't that Mom didn't love her. Breezy didn't have a sad childhood locked under the stairs playing second fiddle Harry Potter to Neve's Dudley. It was that Mom always seemed to see something in Neve . . . some invisible potential that appeared lacking in Breezy.

Extraordinary Neve had enjoyed skating and done well, then worked hard in journalism school in Boulder and made it through the ranks in a tough, demanding profession covering the competitive sports beat.

Breezy worked hard too, but face it, she was a librarian who could barely chew gum and walk in a straight line.

Safe.

Simple.

Uncomplicated.

Ordinary.

Neve and Breezy never discussed their mom's favoritism. What was there to say? Mom had coached group and private kid lessons at a family ice arena in the suburbs for years. Neve had found modest success with the sport while Breezy gave up in favor of reading romance novels in the rink bleachers. Her mother refused to read anything longer than a *Martha Stewart Living* magazine.

They were polar opposites and mostly the knowledge that Mom preferred Neve rolled off Breezy's back. But today it froze like a film of ice.

Because the truth was that Jed West was in *her* house. Helping patch *her* leaky roof. Giving *her* those curious lingering gazes.

Doubt chilled the blood pounding through her heart.

Because it could be that he was just nearsighted. Or she reminded him of someone he couldn't place. Or he thought she was funny-looking.

She tried breathing in, but no dice, her chest was tight with tension. Goddamn it! Her mom was getting in her head, infecting her with a bad case of not-good-enough-itis.

Why couldn't Jed West have been looking at her because he saw . . . *something*, a something that didn't suck. A something that made him stick around for the whole afternoon.

Why couldn't she be good enough to warrant attention from a guy like that?

The anger from when Rory dumped her and her mom didn't look one smidge surprised bubbled up her throat in a molten gurgle. The hurt she swallowed every time Mom read one of her sister's articles—heck, emailed them around to the entire family—but had never visited any of her library events, tightened her throat.

"Mother, you need to leave." The clipped sentence was off her tongue before she could stuff it back inside. Maybe there was no room left.

"Breezy." Mom's fingers literally clutched her twenty-four carat ice skate necklace.

"I'll see you at the picnic." An invisible *good day, sir* exclamation hung in an invisible word bubble over her head.

Mom's brows squashed. "Don't start—"

"My vision isn't what it used to be, but I think we're looking at a grown woman," Granny Dee said sagely. "One in her own home who is calling her own shots. I suggest we respect that."

The stunned silence that followed had its own roar.

Mom straightened her posture and stalked out the door, for once surprised enough not to insist on the last word.

When the door slammed shut, Breezy turned and drew a deep, shuddering breath. The frame on the top of the closest bookshelf read Mirror, Mirror on the Wall, I am Sexy, Screw You All. She glanced down at her leggings.

They were so pants.

The floorboard creaked and she swiveled her head.

Jed West stood in the doorway.

Her world still existed, as ordinary as ever. And yet somehow everything had changed.

Chapter Six

JED ROCKED ON his heels. It wasn't entirely clear what went down between Breezy and her family, and in the grand scheme, it shouldn't matter. At least not to him. He'd meant to come in, rattle off a quick excuse and get the hell out of Dodge. That, of course, was the most intelligent course of action. This afternoon had been a distraction. That's all that was going on here. A fun little break from stressing about whatever was wrong with his fucking head. He had drama enough in his own world. No need to forage for more.

He ran a hand up the rough side of his beard before smoothing it back down. Anyway, he couldn't seriously be considering asking out a *librarian*, could he? What the hell would they even have in common? If her stacked bookshelves were any indication, she was as avid a reader as her profession suggested. In a good year he made it through a couple of audiobooks.

She walked into the kitchen. "Hey."

But the second his gaze locked back on hers, the attraction simmering in his gut rose into a roiling boil. The rules were changing and he didn't know this new game.

Triumphant color blazed across her cheeks and he recognized a moment of victory when he saw one.

Jesus. She was stunning.

"Sorry to make you get up close and personal with my kitchen," she said, waving a hand at her cluttered counter.

"I was going to compliment you on your stand mixer," he replied. *Stand mixer?* What the actual fuck was coming out of his mouth? Worse still, he kept right on going. "I have the same model back at my place, but in silver."

"A Kitchen Companion?" A puzzled furrow appeared between her brows. "You like to cook?"

He leaned against the doorway, crossing his legs with a casualness he didn't feel. "It relaxes me. Plus food on the road sucks most of the time."

She laughed. "That mixer is one of my prized possessions. I own most of the attachments."

"Me too."

She arched a brow. "The ravioli maker?"

He folded his arms. "Used it last Sunday afternoon making kick-ass rosemary sweet potato ravioli."

They stared at each other for a drawn-out moment. He should be leaving, not swapping recipes like Julia Child, and definitely not guesstimating how the weight of her breasts would feel in his upturned palms.

This situation was turning into a gong show, but his feet refused to budge.

"I ordered the ice cream maker this week, should be here any day," she continued.

"It's worth it. I whip up these old-fashioned ice cream sandwiches so good that it would make you think you've died and tasted heaven."

Her lips parted and he could swear her shoulders quaked. "I believe you."

A flash of her naked, spread on his sheets, biting into one popped into his mind. A dribble of vanilla ice cream sliding over the sweet curve of her breast. Licking her to a clean polish.

"I make a batch once a week when I'm home." He cleared his throat. "Do the vanilla bean ice cream on the slowest setting. Then slap it between two fresh-baked chocolate chip cookies."

"Jed West the baker." She appeared to have lost the ability to blink. "Got to say, I'd never have taken you for that."

"What did you take me for?" He'd hate for her to think of him as a high-paid meathead.

Instead of answering, her gaze dropped to the car key clutched in his hand. "Oh." She made a small face, ducking her chin. "Look at me, jabbering away when you must have a lot to do. And, yeah, so, okay then. Thank you for everything." She stepped forward, extending her hand. "It was nice to meet you. Unexpected, but good. Really good."

Instead of giving her a simple handshake, he laced his fingers with hers. Her skin was soft and smooth against his rough calluses. "My pleasure." And that's when the truth hit him with the force of a cartoon anvil.

This afternoon had been nothing but pleasure. Even patching her leaky roof. Meeting her strange relatives. Talking about appliances.

For these past few hours he hadn't been famous, or stuck on a pedestal, which was good because being alienated got old. So did getting treated differently just because he happened to do a job he loved.

Nor did he have that low-grade stress that had been dogging him since his head injury. His fears about karma.

None of it. Instead, he felt . . . normal.

For so long he'd fought tooth and nail to be extraordinary. The best of the best. A champion. But an ordinary heart beat in his chest, one that yearned for simple things. A home, not a high-rise condo with a fridge empty except for beer and protein shakes.

The air vibrated as if someone had struck a tuning fork. She let him go first, releasing him in slow inches before wrapping her hands over her chest, hugging herself. "Guess I'll be seeing you around."

He cocked his head, peered harder. Screw the double

vision, this was like trying to read invisible words between the lines. "You will?"

"Um. Yeah." She mashed her lips, trying and failing to stamp out a flicker of amusement. "Not sure if you've noticed but your face happens to be on about a jillion billboards, plus that new commercial."

"Ah. That cereal one." He glanced to the door. He knew what would happen if he walked out. He'd head to the gym. He'd take out this mounting sexual frustration on free weights. Do a few seven-minute miles. Sweat the poisons out.

"Sorry. Let me get that." She jumped to the door, mistaking his confusion for a sign to leave.

Shit. He didn't want to go, but he didn't know how to be a fucking normal guy. He gave her a curt nod and slung on his jacket. "Goodbye, Breezy Angel." He stepped over the threshold.

"Goodbye, Jed West."

And just like that, the door snicked shut. He turned and strode to the edge of the porch, rain came down hard, the sky breaking open. A strengthening wind stole through his sweatpants, the coolness on his tensed quads a stark contrast to the snug warmth of the cottage to his back. He flipped up his hood. A quick wet dash to his Land Rover and he'd be on his way, racing back to his real life.

It wasn't a conscious thought that caused the pivot. He was knocking before fully registering what he'd done. The door swung open and she leaned against the frame, brow wrinkled with uncertainty. "Forget something?"

"Yeah." He stepped forward, catching a whiff of her shampoo's perfume, the sweet coconut. "I've got a question."

"Shoot." Her two top teeth fastened to her lower lip.

"What's it like?" He reached for a tousled wave escaping her top knot and coiled the lush strands around his finger with a gentle tug. "Kissing that pretty mouth?"

A shy gleam flared in her eyes. "Some mysteries you can never unravel unless you try."

He took her smiling answer as his cue and drew her close, bending her head against the crook of his arm.

Her surprised, husky laugh ended in a breathless sigh that hit him someplace deep inside the chest. He slowed, offering her nothing but a gentle press of lips, innocent, sweet, not even a hint of tongue. She tasted like tea and toothpaste.

Reaching out, she cupped one of his cheeks, tracing a thumb over his scruffy jawbone and he suppressed a shudder.

Way he saw it, there were two choices. Ravage her in the doorway in full view of her entire neighborhood or pull back and take a breath, figure out how the fuck the chastest kiss he'd had since the ninth grade just rocked his goddamn world off its axis.

Of course, he knew what it was to want a woman—how to satisfy and get satisfaction in return. But as her lips tentatively parted, deepening the kiss, a new kind of hunger grew within him, sweetly ravenous. This was a mouth a man could lose himself in. But could he afford to get more confused than he'd been of late? The only way he succeeded in his world was to anticipate the next three steps ahead.

That game seven hit and the resulting ramifications sure as shit hadn't been in the cards.

And Breezy Angel? He'd wanted to know what it was like to kiss her, had suspected it would be good, hoped for great. But as far as firsts went in his life, it was un-surpassed.

He pressed her up in the doorway, a hint of grind to his hips, wanting, no—needing—those perfect tits crushed to his chest. She was a wild card. He dipped his hands to frame her flared hips, the dip to her hourglass waist.

"You'd better come back inside," she said breathlessly.

"Good idea." He hiked her up by the waist and slammed her center against his growing bulge. Less thinking, more doing. Her eyes widened in surprise as he reached down, finding purchase under her thighs. Stepping inside, he back-kicked the door before turning her around and crushing her into the wood.

Oh, hell yes. He loved having her weight in his arms, all that decadence in all the right places—voluptuous and heady. All woman. As she wriggled in closer, lock-ing her ankles at the small of his back and gripping his shoulders hard, his control snapped and they sank to the floor.

She explored beneath his sweatshirt. Her fingers were cool, but that wasn't what caused his goose bumps. She glanced down at the inches of bare abdomen sneaking beneath his Under Armour, flexed and rigid, and a small moan escaped her parted lips. A fierce pride lit within. All those hours punishing his body, making it hard, invincible, like a modern-day gladiator, had paid off.

She reached out as if to stroke his external obliques and paused, uncertainty on her features. "Sorry, I'm getting handsy."

"That's the whole idea here, Vixen." The nickname slid off his tongue. She was foxy as hell, all curves and chaos. "Go on, get closer. A little bit closer. Yeah." He pressed his nose against her neck. "Christ, you smell fantastic."

Her hands fisted his hair. He'd been meaning to cut it for summer but right now was glad it was shaggy. It hurt fucking good.

"Jed." The desperate way she whispered his name drove him wild. His name. Not West or Westy. Just Jed.

Her next kiss was more possessive, almost aggressive. She plundered and he allowed her to take the lead, let her fuck him with her tongue until his heart near burst from his chest.

"Jesus." She whispered over and over. "Oh *Jesus.*"

"No one's answering those prayers but me," he growled, clamping her full ass, dragging her over his pelvis. "You're slumming with the sinners now, Ms. Angel." He broke the kiss and nibbled along her neck as she writhed, pulling his hair, rocking like a devil over his growing erection. The cotton from her pants and his sweats added a layer of friction. He hadn't dry humped since high school, but it felt as intimate as if they were buck-ass naked and coated in oil. His stomach churned, his balls drawn up heavy and sensitive. "You're something else, Breezy Angel."

"I don't know what I am," she whispered, unsure if he heard as he tenderly assaulted her neck, his tongue skimming, his teeth nipping, lifting her to unbearable heights.

WHOEVER GOT A shot with their wildest fantasy? No one, that's who. And better yet, here she was getting exactly that.

"Hey," he breathed, pulling back, cupping her cheeks, forehead resting against hers.

"Hi." She let her lids fall shut and just existed. "Be in the present," was one of those nauseatingly pragmatic pieces of advice like drink lots of water or get eight to nine hours of beauty sleep.

Of course it was a sensible idea, but coffee was so delicious and so was wine. And who could go to bed before midnight when there was always another chapter?

But right now, right here, she was in the present and it was good here. So good. The past didn't matter. Neither did the future. Just the now. Just this.

Jed West stroked the soft skin near her temple with his thumb, touching her like she was of value. Precious.

"Let me see those eyes, pretty," he rumbled.

And when Jed West put the sheer force of his will to something, it happened. Her lids sprang open.

"I'd better be careful," he whispered. "I could get lost in there."

She mashed her lips.

"Too cheesy?"

"I happen to love cheese." She kissed the corner of his mouth. Because those were perfect lips. Because she could. "That was a gouda compliment. Get it, good-a? Eh? Eh?"

"That's terrible," he groaned.

"I'm here all night, ladies and gentlemen," she said in a fake late-night host voice.

"Get back over here." He slanted his mouth over her and they didn't come up for air for an hour. Night fell outside the windows. An hour of nothing but kissing and it was easily the hottest encounter of her life. Finally they broke off, panting, entwined and unsure where to take it from here.

"What's that?" he mumbled, shifting to better get an arm around her waist.

"On my shelves? They are called books." They were literally exploding with titles. She'd stacked two more piles on either side of the case. There were classics there, Mark Twain, Jane Austen and Virginia Woolf. But also the entire Sweet Valley High series. And V.C. Andrews. Was he trying to judge her reading because nothing besides someone dissing the Hellions made her feistier.

"I meant the photo." He squinted, rising up on one elbow. "Is that you?"

"Let me guess." She groaned, knowing exactly what he was talking about without looking. "You want to know why I'm skating with a traffic cone?"

"I've seen toddlers do that I think, but . . ."

"I was eight. My mom coached me," Breezy said grimly. "She was actually good back in the day. Really good. Qualified for the U.S. championships back in the seventies good. A couple of years ago she married the Zamboni driver at her rink, my stepdad, Jim. Neve was pretty good too. Didn't go as far as Mom, but had the knack. They bonded over it. Mom made all her costumes."

"What about you?"

"No knack." She shrugged. "No bond. I appreciate skating as a sport. I do. But not going to lie, I suck monkeys at it. I'm good at reading. It's kind of my thing. Sports? Nope. But enough about me and my boring sibling rivalry. Big sister good at everything. Little sister can't keep up. Blah. Blah. Zzzz."

That's when she sensed it. A tenseness. A fidgety unease.

Zzzz was right. This was supposed to be sexy times. She was boring him batty with tales from her sad-sack childhood.

Of course he wanted to go. Could she be any more of a boner killer?

At least she'd get to have bragging rights for the rest

of her life. Fodder for a sassy PG-13 story to be regaled over future family dinners.

Hey, Mom, wanna hear about the time Jed West chose me for an hour of not-so-innocent tonsil hockey. Not Neve. Me!

Yeah. Or maybe she could just keep this little chestnut to herself.

If she sucked the face of a hockey god and no one ever found out, did it actually happen?

She didn't have to consult the Magic 8 Ball perched on the coffee table to know the verdict. *Signs point to yes.*

Someday in the distant future, when she forgot everything, including her own name, she'd still remember the hot press of Jed West's mouth branding over hers. Wow. He could kiss. Those lips deserved one hell of a Yelp review.

But apparently, the satisfaction wasn't mutual. Her stomach cooled at the hooded look in his eyes as his roving glance fixated on the door. The inner fire that had shown on his face was doused.

She'd done something wrong.

Or maybe what he really wanted was someone like Neve or Margot. Someone smaller. More dainty. Who could wear a tank top with no bra and look adorable. She on the other hand was too much. Too big. Too boobalicious. Too bootylicious.

She opened her mouth, but he beat her to the punch. "Listen, I hate to do this . . ."

"You remembered you had to be somewhere?" She

glanced at the ceiling. The storm was quieter now. Less of a rage and more of a mournful trickle. What had she done? Just babbled about being the younger sister, unable to keep up?

He released her and stood, took his time gathering his things. At least he was good at this. Leaving and not looking like an asshole.

She rose herself. Clothes were straightened. Hair smoothed.

"So I gotta . . . There's this thing . . ." He trailed off floundering before jerking that perfect chin to the door, letting that perfectly carved jaw finish the sentence with a curt gesture. "It's important." He nodded twice as if to convince himself, his cheeks flushed.

"Yeah. Totally. Seems like it." It was official. Not just random insecurities floating around her head. He wanted to go. She'd blown it.

Tick. Tick. Tick. The cuckoo clock on her wall, a housewarming gift from Granny Dee, pounded into her skull. *What? What? What?*

Had she slobbered? Had her belly been too soft? Her ass too big.

Insecurity was an ugly thing. It gnawed at the corners. Could consume her alive if she allowed it to fester.

"What are those?" He pointed at one of her four bookshelves on his way to the door.

It took her a second to figure out what he was asking. "Oh. My Funko Pop collection?" Her cheeks grew hot. "It's a silly hobby. I collect characters from some of my favorite books. That's Katniss Everdeen. And that's Jamie Fraser. And that's Harry Potter. Oh, and Voldemort."

"The one next to Harry, doesn't his best friend have red hair?"

"I don't have a Ron. Oh . . ." She trailed off. "That one's Edward. From *Twilight*."

She imagined seeing her fun, harmless little addiction through his eyes. Did it make her look like a crazy cat lady, minus the cats?

"You really do love books." He didn't make it sound like a bad thing, but she still bristled.

Because this was who she was. What she loved. "I adore chocolate. I *require* books. They are like oxygen or water, vital to my existence."

"I see. Anyway, this was nice." He spoke formally, making the abrupt observation as if commenting on the weather, as if they hadn't just spent an hour body-checking each other all over the living room. "This was fun." He ducked in for a formal peck but she had already averted her face. His lips landed in her hair.

Hopefully he got a mouthful. Not that she deserved to be miffed. After all he was Jed West, hockey captain extraordinaire and who was she? Just an ordinary girl who should be damn grateful for this one extraordinary moment.

The worst part was . . . he still didn't leave immediately. Instead, he lingered by the bookshelf. Studied a few titles. Poked her Peeta Funko with something that looked a lot like regret. Good lord, and to think she beat herself up for making things awkward. He gave her a serious run for her money in that department.

More evidence that they were well matched.

It could almost be funny if she wasn't so close to crying.

Then, after heaving a final frustrated sigh, he left, not turning around as he closed the door behind him. She grabbed a throw pillow and balled it to her chest. What was wrong? After all, shouldn't she be giddy for the experience? Grateful for getting a taste of her dream? Not sagging faster than a deflated helium balloon.

All she knew was she was worn-out. Exhausted really.

Bone tired of never feeling good enough.

Chapter Seven

JED WENT HOME and didn't think about Breezy. He didn't think about her while he tossed and turned in his California king-size bed, or got up to grab a glass of water. Not even when he watched some crappy late-night. Certainly not while playing *The Legend of Zelda* on his classic Nintendo NES and dying twice in the same fucking dungeon. Not even when he decided to soak in a piping-hot bath with a single-malt scotch.

It wasn't until his hand migrated down to the erection straining against his abs that he had to own the fact.

Vixen hadn't been out of his head since the second he left.

Instead of taking hold of his shaft, he took his time, pressing his cock down flat, rubbing his head—lightly at first—with one hand while his other squeezed and roughly pinched his nipples. It didn't take long for his raspy groans to echo from the tiled wall. More burned in his belly than the whiskey.

God, Breezy had such a gorgeous mouth and knew how to use it. Not even two tumblers of expensive alcohol could drown out the memory of her sweetness. Her smooth satin skin, the way it flushed under his stubble. He could guess how she'd taste between her legs. The flavor. Nectar. Spring water. Citrus. Salt. Natural.

Addictive.

He'd felt close to her. Then she started talking about disappointing her mother. Living in the shadow of an older sibling.

And that had been . . . too close. Too close for comfort.

He kept up the rhythm, but his body resisted. The lust coiled inside him wasn't a lazy, indulgent need to be wacked out on his back in slow, leisurely strokes. It was sharper. Acute. A type that set his teeth on edge. Made him want to bite down into leather. He pushed all troubled thoughts away and focused on this simple, pure desire.

His tongue had been inside her, deep kissing. Imagine what it would be like to fuck her with his mouth. The vision made him groan out loud. At first her slick inner lips would graze his like the softest of kisses. But it wouldn't take long to turn hot and wet as she ground her hips on his face. He sensed that she was the kind of woman who could let go. Be utterly sexual. Sensual. It was all there coiled and uninhibited. Waiting for someone to flip her lid.

"Ah, shit." He climbed up on the side of the bath, craving the release, the ceramic cool under his bare ass. Water sloshed on the floor as he hunched over, pumping his shaft, the tip of his cock gleaming and not just from the bathwater. With the other hand he rubbed his tight sac. The friction was loud, but not as loud as the grunt he made as his release hit him like a slug in the gut.

After, he sank back into the tub, vaguely unsatisfied. He'd taken the edge off, but the fucking pressure was still there, the desire unspent still pressing inside him, like some wild beast railing against a cage.

"Two days," he muttered, rising from the tub and grabbing a gray Egyptian cotton towel and slinging it around his waist, wincing as it brushed his still sensitive cock. "Give it two days."

His shoulders instantly relaxed. A game plan. Good. Yes. That's what he needed. He'd wait forty-eight hours for the effects of this evening's drug to wear off. If he still felt the same way then he'd call Breezy. But likely this attraction would dissipate and he'd return to normally scheduled summer programming.

And anyway, would she even want to talk to him, when he'd bolted like the king of assholes?

His own dad was a piece of work too. A rigid, intimidating guy who had expected great things from both sons, demanded nothing less than the best in school, in sport, in life. He pitted them against each other, the comparisons constant.

When Jed got moved into remedial English in junior

high, he'd lost ground in the ongoing parent approval competition. That's when he made it his life's mission to surpass his big brother in the rink until finally Travis gravitated to football, hating the fact his younger brother skated harder, faster, left his goddamn guts on the ice. After Travis took off his skates, he never looked back. Got the big scholarship to UCLA. Star receiver as a freshman. Cutting angles to the end zone. Ready to live the dream.

Dad was so fucking proud.

Then came the game sophomore year where Travis slammed his head, his brain smashing the inside of his skull. It rocked his world right into the shitter. He had a full-blown seizure on the field, bled from the mouth. Turned out he'd gotten a concussion in an earlier game a week before. The second impact is what did it. Turned out there was a name for the injury—nothing fancy— second impact syndrome.

They'd chopped open Travis's skull, removed a clot. And that was it. Game over. The brother he had known was gone. In his place remained an angry, erratic man who grasped enough to know that so much had been lost.

But that didn't have to be Jed's story.

His jaw muscles tightened. But why? Why did he deserve to keep winning when his brother, his own flesh and blood, had lost so much? Maybe this was karmic balance finally being restored.

Or a wake-up call.

He didn't have to stick around. If he wanted out, this was the time, having led his team to not one but *two* championships. He had nothing to prove to anyone anymore. Not to Dad. Not to critics.

But what about himself?

He'd hidden behind hockey for so long now, who would he be if he walked away?

And that was the problem. He wasn't sure he wanted to find out.

"Boss?" Daisy used the expression without irony, but the deferential expression still made Breezy smile. "You have a call on line three."

"Take a message?" She peered down from the step stool, halfway through setting up a new display all about the biological diversity of the Rocky Mountains. Right now she was trying to staple a cardboard cutout of a chipmunk, but the darn gun kept jamming. "Got my hands full."

"I tried," Daisy persisted. "But trust me . . . you're going to want to take this."

Breezy glanced back, unsettled by the high-pitched strangeness in her tech's voice.

"What's wrong? Tater Tots ready to start chopping heads?" Jed West's surprise appearance had circulated through the branch, but so far her boss hadn't made any particular mention of the coup.

"Define wrong." Her assistant ogled her like she was

a stranger. "Could it be described as having the captain of the Hellions calling me?"

Breezy narrowly missed stapling her thumb. "Excuse me?"

"*Jed West* is on line three."

Breezy's knees became the consistency of Jell-O. She leaned against the bulletin board and took a steadying breath, trying not to melt off the chair she was standing on.

"You must have left quite an impression the other day."

Images fast-forwarded through her mind. How his stubble grizzled her cheek. How his tongue slid hot and insistent over hers. How freaking adorable he looked doing menial domestic chores. How he sounded when laughing over nerdy high-end kitchen gadgets.

But why call now? It had been two days of radio silence since he'd smooched and skedaddled.

Must have forgotten something. Except that she hadn't noticed any items left behind or they would currently be part of an "Oh Mah Gawd I Kissed Jed West" Altar of Perpetual Thanksgiving in her bedroom.

"I'll be right there." She took a breath and stepped down.

An unreasonable hope flickered, but she blew it out before it could become much more than a spark. No way was he actually interested, right? In her?

And yet here she was, belly tight and breasts aching and heavy. And it wasn't because he was so hot that he made trees look for shade. For years she'd lusted after him. The perfect fantasy. The Viking-strong body. The lickable jaw. The shiver-inducing voice. The hero.

But what about the guy behind the fantasy? He was a good one. Great actually. The whole package. Nice. Funny and sweet. She'd once read that he'd been an Eagle Scout, and after meeting him in person, of course he had been.

But the first rule of crushing hard on someone who is unattainable is admitting the truth. She was lucky to play with fire. But she had to be smart not to get burned.

As she walked to the desk, the reasons for his call ran through her mind. Sex? Or maybe silence.

Ah. She nodded to herself. That one made sense.

He was notoriously tight-lipped about his personal life. No doubt he wanted to make sure she didn't go sharing details of their hookup with Neve, having it leak into the press.

At least she could honestly admit she hadn't told a soul.

She wasn't sure why. Bragging rights on such a stunt would be a beautiful thing. Her family cred would spike off the charts.

She reached her desk and stood, hand hovering over the phone, and licked her dry lips. The little light blinked on line three.

I wanted to be special. A stupid feeling. An indulgent impulse. But their kissing had felt like a real moment. And if he did this sort of thing a lot, well, she didn't. Hadn't.

What did he want?

Only one way to find out. Time to harness the power of her ovaries and get this over with.

"Hello? This is Breezy." For once she lived up to her name.

"Hi. It's me. Jed. West, J-Jed West."

Her heart started to pound. She recognized an awkward verbal stumble, she was a master herself.

"Can I help *you* with something for a change?" Her hand trembled, then her teeth joined the party with an audible chatter. It was as if the room had dropped to minus twenty, crazy considering she was overheating. A small bead of sweat trickled under her bra strap, down the small of her back.

"Yes. I. Okay." He cleared his throat. "I have to get a present for a child. And he is a boy. This particular child. And a, uh, big reader like you. I'm wondering if you have any notable recommendations."

"Age?"

"Uh, eight."

"What does he like?"

"I don't know."

"You want a book recommendation for a child you don't know?"

"I know the child. He's my nephew. But we're not close. We don't see much of each other and I don't know much about kid books. I didn't read much at his age."

She was a reader, not a writer, but knew enough from that tight tone to understand there was a story there.

"Let's simplify. Funny or adventure?"

"You choose."

"What about *Tales of a Fourth Grade Nothing*? It's by Judy Blume. Long-suffering brother facing off against a seriously pesky little brother. It's usually a big hit among that age demographic."

"Tales of a . . . Fourth Grade . . . Nothing." He repeated back slowly as if he was writing it down. "Great. Thank you."

"No, thank you." She winced. God, could she sound dumber? "Glad I could be of help."

"You take care now."

"Okay?" That was it? "Bye?" Wait, seriously? That was literally why he had called?

There was a silence.

Click.

Well, then.

She hung up and glanced to the Westy calendar pinned to her cubicle wall. "What the hell? Do you not have access to Google and working fingers?"

Before she could begin what was sure to be a long and eventful obsession session, the phone rang again. She startled at the sharp ring.

"Hello, children's desk. This is Breezy."

"Me again."

She twisted the phone cord around her finger. "Let me guess. This time you want a recommendation for a little girl. Six. Just mastering sight words."

"No. I wanted to see what you were doing tomorrow. It's why I called."

She rocked her head back and mouthed a *thank you* to the ceiling. Threw in a thumbs-up for good measure. And a promise to be more attentive to recycling. "So there is no little boy."

"No. There is. But Josh was my foot in the door."

As if he needed a reason. He was Jed freaking West. She was Breezy "can't even keep Rory Munge interested" Angel.

"Was that wrong?" he asked, testing the silence.

She nibbled her bottom lip. "Only if it's wrong that I'm flattered."

"I won't tell if you don't." The smile was evident in his own voice. The sound heated her ear. "So about tomorrow."

Ugh, tomorrow.

"I'll be getting pecked to death by ducks. At least it's going to feel that way. I have to go to this Angel Annual Fourth of July picnic. You met two of them. Sharp beaks."

"Family thing?"

"One of many. Quality time is big on Mom's side. But . . . hmm . . . how can I put this nicely, they can be a lot to deal with." Aka Aunt Shell would drink too much hard lemonade and try discussing politics with anyone in an eighty-foot radius. Mom would follow Neve around encouraging her to eat because she was "skin and bone" while making a *tsk* sound every time Breezy reached for anything from a carrot on the veggie platter to a whole pie to face-plant in.

"Want backup?"

Her heart skipped a beat. "That all depends on the who, what and why."

"Me, by your side, because I'd like to get to know you better."

"My sister will be there too. *Neve.*" Ah, there she went. Dangling her sister's name to see if he'd bite.

"I like Neve." A pause. "But got to say, I like you more."

It was official. She'd burn in some sort of terrible, disloyal sister hell for the amount of joy that simple sentence brought her.

"I have to arrive by three. Can't be late on pain of death. I'm bringing the flag cake. I don't mean to brag but it's probably the reason at least half of my family is going to be on time. It goes fast."

"I'm intrigued."

"You've seen my badass kitchen mixer. I don't mess around." She barely recognized herself. This bold, confident woman getting sassy and a little sexy on someone who to any outside observer was a solid ten to her average five.

"Now that's a lie," he rumbled. "Because you've been messing with my head for forty-eight hours."

"Wow." She crossed her legs and plucked the phone cord. "That might be the worst pickup ever."

"Nah. That would be the GMC Syclone. Can't tow with it. Has limited payload and no chance of ever going off-road."

She smiled at their banter. "Sounds like you're talking from experience, wise guy."

"That piece of crap was my first truck. Dad bought it off a neighbor who was too ashamed to own it a day longer."

Another fun fact to file away on Jed.

She had so many already.

Her half smile faded to a full frown. That was a little weird actually, knowing so many random tidbits about his life.

Especially when he didn't know any of that.

But how exactly does one break out with: *Hey, so . . . Jed . . . you might find this funny, funny weird rather than haha, but see, I'm your biggest fan. And don't let that put you off or anything because I'm prepared to focus on the real you rather than the legend.*

He'd run screaming for the door.

Anyway, she hadn't technically said she didn't like hockey. It was more like an omission. If a miracle happened and she and Jed were ever to start something, that's when she'd tell him. When the moment was right.

All she knew right *now* was that their chemistry was mad-scientist-cackling-in-the-laboratory insane. And on top of the fact she wanted to eat his face every time he glanced her direction, she wanted to also just hang out. Make ice cream sandwiches and homemade ravioli. Joke around. Laugh.

"One last thing." Because there was one thing she couldn't omit in good conscience. "You do remember that the women in my family are hockey crazy? If you go, I can't promise that it won't come up. But even though they are all a little nuts, they are good people." Her people. And she wanted Jed to like them too, or at least actively tolerate their quirks.

"Can't wait. I'll see you tomorrow."

"Sounds good." What it sounded like was holy fucking shit what is life but that didn't seem like the best idea to share. "Looking forward to it."

Understatement of the year.

Chapter Eight

JED PARKED HIS Land Rover on the shady street in front of the old brick home decorated in red, white and blue bunting. By the time he'd climbed out and gotten to the passenger door, Breezy was climbing out.

"Did you need something?" She raised her brows, hands clasping the cake pan wrapped in plastic cling wrap.

"I dunno." He closed one eye and kicked a broken piece of asphalt. "Just to feel like a gentleman?"

It took her a second to work out his meaning. She glanced between the car, to him and back before a light-bulb went off. "Oh. Oh! You were going to let me out of the car? Well, then, hang on." She opened the door and climbed back inside. "By all means, proceed."

Was she mocking him? He frowned the thought away. She didn't seem like the type to bust his balls. Then again, the only things he could say about Breezy Angel with any degree of certainty was that she liked a wide variety of sex toys, had a laugh that he wanted to hear again and again, a great ass and an authentic quality.

A refreshing realness.

"What are you doing?" he questioned as she pulled the passenger door shut.

She leaned against the window. "No one has ever opened my car door before," she shouted. "Not a once. There's no way that I'm missing out." The glass fogged from her breath and she drew a smiley face in the condensation.

While her eyes danced with amusement, he knew with the same confidence that he knew that the first NHL goal was scored on December 19, 1917 by Dave Ritchie of the Montreal Wanderers against the Toronto Arenas that she was being dead serious.

Which was fucking crazy.

No guy had ever opened Breezy's car door? What was wrong with his gender? Talk about a pack of morons.

But he didn't have time to nurse the flash of irritation. Not when she was looking at him expectantly, like having him perform a small chivalrous gesture, like opening her car door, made him the white knight of her dreams.

This was a girl who believed in fairy tales. He could do this small thing for her.

He grabbed the door handle and opened it. She flopped back in her seat and smiled. "Again."

"What?"

"Please do it one more time?" Her laugh was damn charming. "Really let me savor the moment."

Now he felt like laughing too, at the pure adorable idiocy of the situation.

He complied with her request, sweeping into a low bow as he helped her outside. Once she was standing, he leaned close, lips hovering against the edge of her ear. "How was that?" He inhaled her clean scent. "Live up to every expectation?"

"And then some." Her body responded in a subtle shiver as he pulled back. Her gaze dropped to his mouth and her lips parted as if she wanted to say something more, but hesitated.

The silence felt loud with all the things that were going unsaid. Their drive here hadn't been quiet. There'd been music. Pleasantries exchanged. But nothing that dived below the surface. Certainly no acknowledgement of their kissing marathon. Or the fact he'd bolted for the door.

"They're here! They're here!" A child's voice cried from the open door. Excited chatter rose from inside.

Breezy winced, even as a smile appeared. "That's my cousin Sam. He's nine, the baby in the family. You sure you're up for this? My family . . . I wasn't kidding, they are a lot."

His own family was small. His mother was an only child and his father had lost his younger brother in a car accident while still a young man. He knew his parents loved him, but they weren't the type to say it. Instead he'd hear his father bark "you didn't try enough," every time Jed lost a game in high school.

It got so bad Jed asked him to stop coming to his games, even though he almost always won. Losing still sucked. And to have your dad up on the bench, his face long with disappointment, made it ten times worse. Dad didn't say much after Jed's frustrated request. But after that the focus doubled down on Travis.

And he'd let that happen. Been relieved even.

He froze, realizing Breezy had just asked him a question and he didn't have the first clue what it was about.

"Can you repeat that?"

"I was just wondering if your family does get-togethers?"

"Nah." Hopefully his shrug looked natural. "My big brother lives in Oakland with his wife and kid. And my parents live in the Bay too. But everyone tends to keep to their individual silos."

"Ah." She considered his explanation. "I'm trying to decide if that sounds sad or relaxing. What about Christmas and stuff?"

He frowned. Last year his parents had gone on a cruise in Egypt, on the fucking Nile. The Nile. Denial. That joke had been almost funny after a beer . . . or six.

"Usually I just hang out with Tor . . . I mean, Coach Gunnar. He's divorced and we used the holiday breaks to catch up on reviewing game tapes."

Breezy got that look on her face again. The one that seemed to want to call bullshit, but was too polite.

"Oh say can you see . . . someone gorgeous is in front of me." Granny Dee's warbling voice rang out as she draped in the doorway wearing a shirt that read Party Like It's 1776 and winked from under a giant Uncle Sam hat.

If Granny noticed them jump apart, she didn't let on. "Fancy seeing you twice in one week, handsome." She made a show of looking around. "Tell me you brought that Patchy Donnelly, please? Please?"

"Sorry, ma'am, I don't have much communication with him in the off-season." He wasn't close to Patch. Goalies were notoriously difficult personalities and Donnelly wasn't much different in that department.

"That's a shame, that boy is . . ." Granny Dee glanced down at Sam before clicking her tongue and made a Campbell's Soup "mmm, mmm, good" sound.

"What?" Sam looked up between the adults, scratching the side of his snub nose. "What's that mean?"

No one was brave enough to answer.

"Come in, come in." Granny seized their arms and dragged them inside. "Most folks are out on the back porch."

"They're eating already?" Breezy asked. "I brought the flag cake."

Jed eyed the sheer number of shoes lined by the door. Just how many people were here?

"Don't shoot the messenger." Granny Dee shrugged. "Now about you. Big man like you must have one heck of an appetite. You want a burger, Westy? Or a hot dog? There's ribs going too. And three different kinds of chili. Each of my sons-in-law thinks they've got the perfect recipe. But they're all wrong. Nobody can match me."

"That's not false modesty," Breezy murmured, leaning in. "No one is absolutely sure how she does it, but it's good. Better than good."

The noise from the backyard was deafening. Sounded like everyone was having a good time. Jed hesitated, not wanting to go in and mess up the dynamic. Conversation would grind to a halt. People would point and whisper.

"Tell you what, I'll take a glass of water," he told the grandmother. It was hard to look her straight on in that hat.

"Water? That I can do. Take out the cake, Bumper Butt, and make your uncles happy. I'll hydrate Westy and see if he wants to help Sam with his board game."

"Board games?" Breezy pulled up tight. "Weren't those uniformly banned from Angel parties after the fight two years ago?"

"After the Monopoly fight?" Granny asked.

"When Aunt Lo head-butted Uncle Spence!"

"Well she's into transcendental meditation now. And this is The Settlers of Catan."

"It's long," Sam announced. "That's all I know. The grownups want to keep me occupied."

Breezy frowned at him. "I don't know if Jed is up for long."

"Sounds fun," he said quickly. The real reason he was here was because he wanted to be closer to Breezy. Not because he was interested in socializing with a mass of strangers, especially ones that fight over board games. His family didn't verbalize feelings. You knew Mom was upset if she poured a glass of Chardonnay and went in her bedroom.

"So the rumors are true," a deep voice boomed. An intellectual-looking man with thick black glasses and a trimmed gray beard sauntered down the hall. "All of hell is empty and the devils are here, am I right?" He gave them a look of mock seriousness before booming a laugh and clasping Jed on the shoulders. "What can I get you to drink?"

"I'm grabbing him a water, Spencer," Granny said. "This is my son-in-law. He teaches Shakespeare at the community college."

"Water?" The guy waved her off. "This is Jed West. Get this man a beer. A quart of ale is meal for a king and besides the foolery is in full swing."

"Heya, Uncle Spence, rhyming this early in the day?" Breezy patted the man on the shoulder of his sweater vest before dragging Jed into a hallway alcove. "You don't have to drink or eat anything they try to shove down your throat, nor do you have to play board games with my cousin and ninety-year-old grandma."

"Game sounds good." His vision began to warp

on the edges. It took effort to keep his features steady. "Nice and low-key." At least he could sit and wait for it to pass.

"I'm going to drop off the cake but then I'll be back in fast. You okay?" Breezy gave him a concerned look. "You look a little funny."

"Me? I'm fine. Fine." He'd used the lie so often in his life that he could deliver the untruth smooth and polished, like rock from a tumbler.

The Settlers of Catan turned out to be anything but low-key. Grandma and Sam took their places at a small table in the library, the room lined with wall-to-ceiling bookshelves.

He couldn't read a single title, or the directions that Granny handed him as Sam spoke fast about things like victory cards and hexes, robbers and tokens.

From another room, Breezy's name was called again, this time heavy with intent. Gossip was clearly floating throughout the party, like dandelion fluffs on the breeze.

He suspected he was the source.

Shit. He ground his teeth. He'd wanted to spend more time with Breezy, be normal. But he was kidding himself. There was nothing normal happening here. The slow metronome of his heart began to pick up the tempo.

"I gotta pee," Sam announced with the abruptness of a child.

"I've been waiting for it to be just you and me." Granny leaned in and punched his arm. "Tell me a story."

"A story?" Jed shifted on the plush chair. It was too soft. Hurt his back. "I'm not much of a reader."

"You're funny." She paused to take a noisy sip from her frosty tumbler. "I like it."

The beverage inside was lime colored and icy. His mouth was dry and his stomach felt as small and hard as a walnut.

"I've been trying checking up on you." She swayed a little to the Bruce Springsteen piping in from the backyard. "There's not a lot of juicy material out there."

He nodded. "I'm pretty dry."

"Your love life seems like it." Her gaze was appraising. "Why don't you have a girlfriend?"

"Guess I haven't found the right one." His parents' marriage didn't inspire wild fantasies. Unlike Breezy, he didn't believe in fairy tales. Instead he believed in quiet, strained silences, the din of cable news television drowning out unhappiness.

"Hmm. And family? You see much of them?"

Despite the wrinkles, her eyes were sharp. This wasn't befuddled questioning from an elderly woman. Hell no, this was an experienced bloodhound. There could be little doubt where Neve inherited her skills.

Jesus.

Talk about getting the third degree. He glanced to

the hall and it was empty. Where was Sam? The kid must have a bladder like a camel. And Breezy was nowhere to be seen. It was like being alone with the Godfather.

Part of him suspected that this might not be an accident.

"I wasn't asked in here to play a game, was I?"

Granny's eyes widened even as they glinted. "Whatever do you mean?"

He leaned forward, clasped his hands and set them on the table. "Mrs. Angel—"

"Good lord, son, don't call me that. Makes me think my mother-in-law is back from the dead and standing behind my shoulder." She gave a visible twitch. "That woman was a dragon lady of the highest order, although I don't like to speak ill of the dead. Now, please, Granny Dee. That's what family and friends call me. And I'd like to think we could be friends."

This wasn't how he expected the day to go. Although again, what did he expect?

So might as well roll with it. He rubbed his temple. It wasn't one of the headaches per se. More a twinge. An ache. Right where he'd been hit. His vision smearing continued without any sign of improving.

"I'm a straight shooter, Mrs . . . uh . . . Granny." Despite his best effort, his voice was strained. "If you have something you want to say. Hit me." He fought for a grin. "I've got experience in that department."

"Don't I know it. You're not one of the flashy players, but you're one hell of a workhorse. Good instincts, one of the best shot blockers in the league. But we can talk shop another time. Right now I want to know what a guy like you is doing with Breezy."

He frowned. "What's that supposed to mean?" He bristled.

"You don't think she's a little . . . ordinary for the likes of you?"

The memory of her weight in his arms. Her kisses on his lips. The way she made him feel warm, anchored, actually in his body rather than floating along rose within him. That big hair and bigger smile.

"That's the last word I'd use to describe her, ma'am."

"Go on." Granny slid her drink over. "Have a sip, sonny. Before you burst a blood vessel."

He picked it up and took a long swallow. That's it. This vision problem had been hanging around for too long. He'd have to ball up and make an appointment to see a neurologist.

"I call it the Greenie Meanie. Made it up myself. Like it?"

"Yeah." He wheezed. It was stronger than jet fuel. Christ, this woman must have rum instead of blood in her veins. No wonder she was so well-preserved.

"You're a good man, Jed West. And one hell of a hockey player. But I'm glad to hear you have an inkling about my Breezy, because let me tell you, she is *extraordinary* and it's high time someone has the brains to notice."

Chapter Nine

———————————————————

IT WAS OFFICIAL. Her family had eaten Jed West. Not literally, after all, there he was standing by the BBQ looking all lovely and muscly, nothing like a gnawed pile of bones. But they'd devoured every second of his time at the party. She'd lost all control of him the second she'd entered the house and realized it would look bad if he stumbled on a photograph of her in face paint screaming at hockey games. So she'd let Granny Dee ferry him away for what was likely a grilling session under the subtext of playing a board game.

In the end, the damage wasn't too bad. Her sleuthing unearthed only two photos on the fridge and she hid those under the fruit bowl, then upended a Hellions Angel group shot from last winter facedown on the mantel.

Each act of subterfuge hit her with a pang. This

wasn't being honest. But she didn't have the right words to tell him the truth without looking like a crazy fan. She was a little ashamed of herself, and a lot afraid of his reaction.

Because what would he say if she confessed her obsession with his image, the sexy, bearded captain of the Hellions.

The version of Jed West that was growing more and more unrecognizable as she got to know Jed West the man.

If she wanted him to stick around, she couldn't give him any more reasons to run, especially when Uncle Spencer would not stop with the Shakespeare jokes and Granny was on her third Green Meanie. She'd just conveniently leave out a few facts, and if he wanted to draw his own conclusion that she didn't like sports, no harm, no foul.

Later she'd tell him. Yes. Yes she would.

If they had a later.

She snuck a second slice of flag cake and shoved a whipped cream-covered strawberry into her mouth, biting down. Chewing, she stared straight ahead, refusing to look over at her mom whose disapproving gaze was burning a hole in the side of her face. Out of spite, she forked off an even bigger bite, this time all cake, and forked it in her mouth.

Jed West was here with her. And she was eating cake.

Take that.

Her swallow felt like a raised middle finger to the status quo.

But even while this small victory felt awesome, she really had no idea what was going on. Halfway through the car ride over here, she'd almost leaned over and grabbed Jed's shoulder, given it a shake and yelled, "Hello? Can you please tell me what is going on? What are you doing here?"

She checked her mouth for crumbs. The truth was that if she wanted to get to know him better, it wasn't going to happen lurking over the dessert table. No, she had to stride over and . . . and . . .

A cornhole game was set up on the lawn.

Yesssssss. Perfect.

She sauntered over to a board, picked up a bean bag and tossed it up and down in her hand. "Hey, Jed," she called, casually. Like oh, yeah, *Hey, Jed. Jedy Jed. Jedmeister. What's up, Jed West.* Aka the dude-she-made-out-with-and-who-drove-her-here-and-is-now-stranded-with-her-crazy-family.

She lobbed a bean bag at his feet, but her aim went wild and knocked off the sunglasses propped on the top of his head.

The entire party fell silent. Proof positive if any was needed that everyone had been silently monitoring the situation.

"Oh my God, I'm so so—"

"That's some arm you've got, Vixen." Jed bent down and picked up his shades with an easy grin.

"Vixen?" she heard Aunt Shell murmur to a table. "Who the heck is *Vixen*?"

"Want to play a game?" she asked quickly.

"With a challenge like that, how can I resist?"

He sauntered over and the crowd resumed their chatter.

She reached out and touched the red mark on his forehead. "Sorry about that. I was cut from the high school softball team. With good reason."

"Their loss. You have power in that arm."

"Sorry about my family too. I know they're a little intense."

He leaned in and brushed her hair back from her ear before whispering, "Make me one promise for the rest of the day."

She shivered at his hot breath on her neck. He smelled a little like cinnamon gum and a lot like heaven. "I never make a deal without knowing the terms."

He chuckled, low and deep. "No apologizing."

She pulled back, raising her eyebrows.

"I'm serious. Not one. Not for the rest of the day."

She nodded, cautious.

"And what are we playing for?"

"Like a prize?"

"Sure, every good competition needs a prize. Tell you what. I win, you tell me what's in your granny's Greenie Meanies."

Her eyes widened. "You drank one? Those suckers are lethal."

"She shared hers with me and it tried to knock me on my ass."

"It's the secret to her longevity."

"Then I'll toast to that. And if you win . . ."

She wrinkled her nose. "Shouldn't I get to name my spoils?"

"You could, but I wouldn't make you do that in front of family."

"I'm not sure I understand." She was half-flirtatious and half-confused. It seemed like he was being a little dirty, and it wasn't like she minded, but she also didn't want to assume . . .

"You win the game and your wish is my command. You do like to play games, don't you, Breezy? You have a lot of . . . toys."

Good lord.

He spoke casually enough. Anyone watching them would think he made a passing observation about the weather, or asked for clarification on the game's rules.

But the glint in his eyes? That was pure devil.

"You're bad," she whispered, her cheeks heating. And that wasn't the only place getting a little warmer. Her toes curled.

He didn't blink. "You've got no idea."

She didn't actually. But if there was a benevolent god, he'd grant her a miracle and the opportunity to discover what hid behind his famous "boy next door" persona.

Soon. She shifted, her jeans slick against her secret skin. *Soon.*

He might have run out the other day. But he didn't look like he was going anywhere now.

They played cornhole for the next hour. "Why do I get the distinct impression you are throwing the game?" She laughed as one of his bean bags landed near the kiddie pool.

He winked. "Because you have a brain."

That's it. If she got any wetter she was going to require a raincoat. Time to hit the road. She'd made an appearance. The flag cake was demolished on the table. The music was a little louder. The laughter a little more raucous as Granny Dee's Greenie Meanies circulated the adult crowd and the kids began to feel the effects of the red soda they'd been guzzling by the plastic cup. Sparklers were brought out. Firecrackers began popping.

"I think this might be our cue to leave," she said as Jed missed his next toss. She'd won 9–1.

"You're the winner. Take me home and decide what to do with me." He said it calmly, not a trace of licentiousness. But those were packing deadly intent. Full of wicked promise.

"I'll g-go grab my bag," she stammered.

She bolted into the house and found her handbag in the first-floor guest room. Coming out she froze, hearing her name.

"I'm telling you, it doesn't make sense," her mom was saying in the kitchen. "Breezy? What's the catch?"

"He called her Vixen," Auntie Shell responded.

"*Vixen*. Like . . ." She made an exaggerated *rawr* sound. "I think he likes her."

"Of course he does. She's nice. Likable. Everyone *likes* Breezy." Mom's snort made it sound like it wasn't a great thing. "Now you know I love my little girl, but she doesn't have an ambitious bone in her body. She'd rather read about life than live it. Something isn't adding up here for me."

Breezy found herself unable to move, not to step forward and call her mom out for always dismissing her, never valuing her interests. Never letting her feel like . . . enough.

But at the same time, she was unable to walk away, to plug her ears and quit listening. It was such a strange experience to hear herself being described so honestly, not filtered by any white lies, just pure unvarnished truth.

For her whole life, she'd been trying to uncover that magical potion that got her mom interested in her accomplishments, in her interests.

So she sucked at skating and her mom loved it. So what? Did that one issue have to be the be all and end all of everything?

If she'd known that as a kid, maybe she would have tried harder. Because as much as she didn't like skating, she disliked having her mom write her off even more. Maybe that's why she embraced hockey as much as she did. It was the one connection they shared, a shaky patch of common ground. Otherwise what did they have to talk about? Mom's pointed comments about some stupid new fad diet that had apparently worked wonders for so-and-so at the gym.

But it was true that they had an unspoken war about skating, about Breezy not trying to succeed in a sport that meant so much to her mother. A long silent battle that wasn't so unspoken now that Breezy could hear her talking shit. Dismissing her.

It hurt.

It wasn't fair.

And there was nothing she could do about it right now.

Because she didn't want to get into it with Mom. Not when she could get into it with Jed.

And right now, that score seemed like the sweetest revenge.

Chapter Ten

"WE'RE GOING. NOW."

Jed glanced down at the hand slotted into his like it belonged there. Glancing up, he locked into a pair of silvery blue eyes that held an expression that he recognized. Determination. They shone like a porch light and he was hit with the uncanny feeling of being home.

Digging into his back pocket he pulled out his car keys. "M'lady. Your chariot awaits. Should we go say our goodbyes?"

"No." She was firm, her chin jutting up a little. "We'll vanish in a puff of smoke."

Something had lit a fire in her. And that's the way he liked it. He was drawn to her even though he had a sense he was going to get burned. No one noticed them driving off into the dusk.

"Hey, that was the turnoff to my house," she called

a few minutes later, her head swiveling as she jerked to attention. "But if you go up here and take a—"

"Not taking you home, Vixen," he said in a low voice.

She turned sharply. "Where are we go—"

"My place." He gripped and regripped the wheel. The only body that had been in his bed for over a year had been his own. If he had a hookup, he preferred to keep it in neutral territory, like a hotel on the road. Or if in town, at the girl's place.

"Oh. I see." But it was clear that she didn't.

He turned on music. A deep beat. Thumping. Hard. Mirroring what was happening inside him. Anticipation had honed his insides to a sharp edge.

Breezy reached out and flicked off the music. The uncomfortable silence that followed filled his ears to a deadening roar.

"I'm waiting," she said quietly.

No more elaboration was forthcoming. He'd pissed her off. That much was obvious from the flush on her cheeks and the crackle in her eyes. And he'd been around the block enough to know that when a woman was angry and not saying why, then his ass was in a world of trouble.

"You'd rather to go home?" he ventured at last.

She made a small huffy noise that might as well be a game show buzzer. Wrong! Next choice.

He eased up on the gas. "Mind helping me out? I'm not great at the whole twenty questions thing."

"Or asking, period."

There was a hint in her testy tone. But shit, he wasn't smart enough to pick up whatever she was selling.

Asking. Asking. Asking. He ran the word through his brain, hoping it would spark some idea. Some dim part of him realized he was panicking, that in his interest to get her home and strip her down to her socks, that he'd forgotten—

"Oh. Shit. I didn't ask if you wanted to come over."

She raised a brow, but didn't disagree.

Ding! Ding! Ding! Ladies and gentleman, we have a winner.

Trouble was, figuring out his blunder only got him to the playing field. This was going to have to be an apology knocked out of the park or he wouldn't be getting to a single base.

She mashed her lips together, probably noticing him over here dithering. He was blowing this harder than a fucking popsicle stand.

There was only one way to salvage this. A straight up, from the heart, no bullshit apology.

He pulled the car over and turned off the ignition. Turning, he reached, taking one of her hands. She didn't recoil. Progress.

"I should have asked you to come over. Not assumed, just because."

"Look, Jed." Her voice quavered on his name. "I get it okay. You're like you or whatever. *You.* Westy. Big deal. And I am so happy to be here with you. I am. It's just . . . being around my mom flushes my self-esteem down the toilet. And then it seemed like you were here, ready to make decisions for me and I felt devalued."

Devalued. The word socked him in the gut. He'd done that. He himself alone.

"That wasn't ever my intention. I don't know how to talk about the hockey shit without sounding like a stuck-up asshole. So I'll do the only thing that I know. Which is to call it like I see it. I'm on television. Yeah. All right. I play a professional sport game watched by lots of people. But I didn't get into this work because I wanted to be a star. I did it for one simple reason. I love the work, or used to. Skating is my life. My passion. It's in my blood. Or at least it has been, for most of my life."

"I'm being touchy. And it's hard to navigate. To be ordinary and to be with you, it takes time to get used to."

"Let me tell you one thing. You need to quit saying that. You don't have a drop of ordinary in you. You couldn't be average if you tried."

Her eyes welled with unshed tears, but her smile was something else. And the knot in his gut relaxed. He had a sense he was forgiven for some of his stupidity.

"You said 'used to.'"

He frowned. "What do you mean?"

"Used to love hockey. You don't feel that way anymore?"

His hand went right to his head, the body language betraying him even as she looked on without a clue. "Slip of the tongue," he lied smoothly. He liked Breezy. A lot. She was a good listener. A smart woman. But he wasn't dropping that steaming pile of shit on her door. And besides, he had to be careful.

Last thing he needed was news of his injury reaching her sister's ears. Jed West decides to leave the sport after one concussion too many? It wouldn't take long for a reporter to do a little digging. Find out about Travis and reduce his private tragedy to nothing but a fucking sideshow. A cautionary tale about the dangers of having kids in sport. Helmet debates. The works.

Travis didn't deserve to be a footnote to the Jed West story.

He'd been dealt enough shit cards.

And anyway, this could all be nothing. The symptoms a molehill, not a mountain.

He dug his thumb into his temple and rubbed. *Please be nothing.*

A slippery warmth skimmed his ear and he froze. While he'd been lost in thought, Breezy had clipped out of her seat belt and crawled over the console.

"Tell me you want to take me home," she breathed.

The little hairs on the back of his neck stood at attention. And his cock woke up fast.

He cleared his throat. "I want to take you home."

His shaft thickened at her throaty giggle.

"And then? What will we do when we get there?"

Her tone was teasing, toying and he fucking loved every syllable.

Turning, he moved fast, grabbing the back of her head, burying his fingers in that silken hair and tilting her face to meet him. He couldn't wait to see what she looked like freshly fucked. "First thing I want to know is this . . ." He gave her a slow, thorough kiss. "Do you taste as good between your legs as you do here?"

She sucked in a ragged breath. The flush in her cheeks crept down her neck and he'd bet a Benjamin that the blush kept right on going. Her creamy skin was so damn responsive. Held nothing back.

Which was good, because he was a greedy bastard. And hungry too.

She retreated a fraction.

"Too much?" he asked. A flicker of doubt lit in his chest. He'd never spoken to a woman like this. Maybe it was a mistake letting her peek into his depraved imagination.

Her hand rose to the corner of her mouth. When she nipped the tip of his pinkie finger, he nearly groaned out loud. There it was again. That fucking adorable giggle that made him want to fuck her sideways.

"Mr. West, I do declare." She feigned an innocent Southern accent. She pointed forward. "Drive."

He hit green lights the whole way home.

Jed parked in the condo's private garage and barely got her into the kitchen. "Want the grand tour now, or later?"

"I'll settle for the grand tour inside your pants."

He shook his head, laughing. "You're going to hell, Miss Angel."

"That's fine." She wound her arms around his neck

and ran her tongue along the edge of his jaw. "Long as you burn with me."

One thing was clear. He was going to be coming in his pants like a teenage boy if he didn't act fast.

"You have too many clothes on," He fumbled with her jean button.

"Wait." She grabbed his wrists. "Stop."

The word froze him in an instant. He was dying and ready for salvation, but if she wasn't ready . . . "What's up?"

She bit into her top lip and drew in her brows. "I'm not wearing underwear."

"You're shitting me."

"No shitting." Her face blazed. "I was distracted about seeing you again. I forgot until I got to the bathroom at Aunt Shell's place."

He hooked his thumbs into the waist of her pants. "Then you're killing me." And offered up quiet thanks that his eyes were still working fine. This had gone so far beyond a distraction that he didn't even know where he was anymore. But as she rose up on her knees, giving him space to lower her pants, he suspected it might be heaven. Another inch and another and oh, yeah. Definite heaven.

She was bare. Pink pussy perfection.

"You're staring," she murmured.

"Got that right." If he had a magnifying glass he'd use it. She was peach soft, and there was only one thing to do with such ripe fruit. "I'm gonna eat you."

"Excuse me?" Her head jerked with surprise. Her breath came faster and Christ, he could smell her excitement. She wanted it.

Almost as bad as him.

"You heard me." He leaned back on his elbows, dick throbbing. "Climb on my face, cowgirl. Let's see what you got."

Chapter Eleven

SHE'D NEVER HAD sex on the floor, never mind the floor of an unfamiliar condo with a near total stranger who also wasn't a stranger because she'd fantasized about him so much it felt as if she'd known him for years.

Except she hadn't.

He'd just ordered her to ride his face. Technically, she'd won their game, and was in charge of what happened next, but when Jed West called the shots, every cell in her body was more than happy to obey. She kicked her jeans off from around her ankles, her stomach coiling in anticipation.

It wasn't until she got situated into position that the doubt set in.

Holy crap, he looked perfect between her legs, the honey yellow flecks in his eyes, the hot-as-hell grizzle of

scruff against her inner thighs. The smattering of freckles across his forehead.

If she could take a shot and immortalize it on Instagram without getting cited for pornography she'd post it
with hashtags like #winningatlife or #dreamscancome-
true or for Margot's benefit . . . #magiccarpetride.

If her mom could see her now, she'd know that Jed
didn't prefer her sister. Except it was a very, very good
thing that her mother couldn't see her now.

Self-doubt gnawed at her. Because what was he
seeing? Her sagging belly? Did her boobs look too big at
that angle? What about her thighs?

But then he spread her open with two thick thumbs,
more exposed than she'd ever been, and lapped her
center with a slow, aching circle, and they locked eyes
and something clicked.

He wasn't cataloging her faults. He was here, appre-
ciating, wait, even more than that. He might be a god,
but tonight he worshipped her.

"That's it, honey. Keep your eyes on mine." He sucked
harder, as if drawing her soul from her clit.

All up, not a bad way to go.

On and on it went, his mouth working her over in
tight, tiny circles, his hooded gaze fixed on hers the
whole time. When her inner muscles gripped, her
hips pumping helplessly, his big hands framed her ass,
urging her to ride rougher, gallop past insecurity, until
she was free to take everything he gave. The lace from

her bra put too much pressure on her aching breasts. She slid her hands over the curves, teasing her nipples, trembling when he growled in approval, the vibrations from his mouth radiating through her thighs.

"God." She was so close. And he was so relentless. Wet. Deep.

She wanted to get there, to the desperate edge, to come harder than she had in her life. In the way she was made for, but that no one had ever demanded. But she didn't want to get there alone. He had to be there too.

"What else do you need?"

She gasped, dancing on the edge of her sanity. "Let me get you off too." She twisted as if to dismount, but his fingers dug in, locked her in place.

"Vixen, you already are. I got the best view in the house. Pull your hair up and show off those big, beautiful tits." He groaned as she obeyed, playing her body like a maestro. He kept raising the crescendo, but somehow, skillfully, never let the build slip into actual climax.

She squirmed. Her thighs shook. Her arms trembled. She was wound tight. Need stretched all her muscle fibers tight. Her muscles clenched. If she didn't come soon she might actually explode. That was an entirely possible outcome.

"Please," she gasped. "Please have mercy." She was half laughing. Almost crying. So turned on that it was possible she'd pass out or pass into some strange twilight orgasmic zone.

"Shit," he pulled back. "I can't wait anymore."

"If you did, I might die." She might sound teasing, but was dead serious.

"Nah, Vixen." His eyes were dark, hooded and hot. "But if I do my job right, you're gonna think you've gone to heaven." He moved suddenly, sat up and stood, scooping her to him with superhuman strength. She wasn't a delicate feather, but he didn't even grunt.

Well he did. But in an entirely different way.

She slung her arms around his neck, locking them into place. "Where are we going?"

"When I have you the first time, I'm doing it right," he growled. "In my own bed."

She heaved a happy sigh.

He arched a brow as he walked, amused. "You like that?"

"You said the first time." They ducked into a room. "That means there's going to be a second."

Laughter rumbled through his chest, a deep baritone boom. "Greedy girl."

She didn't have time to study the surroundings. Only register that his spicy masculine scent intensified and that the walls were painted a warm gray. A Hellions jersey hung framed over a black leather chair.

He tossed her on the bed, crawling over her before she'd had a chance to regain her breath. "Tell me." He nuzzled her neck, sucking the sensitive skin as she arched, her breasts pressed tight against his hard slabs of muscle. "You want me to get inside that pretty pussy?"

Oh, lord. He was going to make her ask for it.

She nodded. "Mmm-hmm."

His grin turned wicked as he leaned down and licked the hollow of her throat before blowing on it softly. "Say please."

Scratch that, he was going to make her beg.

Little did he know that she was more than ready to crawl over broken glass, up a hill, in a blizzard as lava, ash and hellfire rained down.

"Pretty," she whimpered, "please on a caramel fudge strawberry banana split with five cherries on top."

He tugged open a drawer on the side table. She didn't look down. Didn't stare as he tugged down his boxer briefs to reveal his thick cock, opened the foil or slid the condom on. It was as if a perfect spell had been cast. She was afraid to move—to breathe—or the moment might disappear faster than a soap bubble.

Instead, she studied the small vein on his right temple. The one that made an appearance on television during stressful games, that one that indicated he was determined. That the other side was about to get destroyed. Except this time she was the opponent, and the idea of getting destroyed never felt so much like winning.

He held himself over her, bracing his torso on his forearms while his lower half sank onto her, hot and heavy. The hard swell of his cock nudged at her center. "You want this?" He bent, searching out her lips, breathing the question into her mouth. "All of me?"

Her throat constricted so tight that speech was impossible. The "yes" came out a muffled whimper as she gave a frantic nod and opened her legs, hands pressing on his lower back, right at the top of his rock-hard ass. Begging him to quit toying. To get closer. To hold nothing back. To be hers.

He didn't enter, instead he rolled his hips in a shallow thrust that did nothing to quench her need. Her heart clanged. "Jed," she gasped. "Jed, please."

As if sensing she was about to fall apart based on pure anticipation alone, he gave in with a slow, decisive lunge. A half smile played on his lips even as the cords on his neck drew tight, but he never closed his eyes. No, they burned her inch by inch until she was consumed, burning from the inside out.

He held himself there, buried to the root, so deep it was impossible to say where her body ended and his began. Sweat slicked his chest, his body heat intensifying the cedar scent of his aftershave as feverish blood thrummed through her own veins. Everything was this moment and yet it was as if she'd drifted somewhere new, beyond time or reason. As short as a breath, as long as a lifetime.

It was Jed who did this to her. Jed West. The man she'd lusted over for years from afar, separated by television screens or stadium seats, and her own starstruck awe.

But he was so much more than Jed West, hockey star. He was simply Jed, a man stripped to nothing but pure animalistic need. Need for *her*.

How extraordinary.

Extraordinary that in his arms she was anything but ordinary. Not an easy lay to be used and discarded. The way he stared down at her was full of wonder, reverence, as if he couldn't believe *his* luck.

In fact, he shuddered. Not a lot. But as he eased out his cock and then buried it again in a tender push, a jolt ran through him. He was taking the moment achingly slow. Savoring it—no, scratch that, more specifically, savoring *her* like a delicious tiramisu, his last meal on Earth.

"Fuck," he groaned softly. "Fuck, Breezy. So good." His breath fell hot upon her cheek as he wrapped his big hands around her thighs, thumbs spreading her lips, and took his time: stretching, feeding himself inside inch by incredible inch until he had nothing more to give.

Until she'd taken everything and was filled, hips arching and heart brimming.

A dark lock of hair tumbled over his forehead. "Hey."

The single word of greeting was so unexpected that a breathless giggle erupted from her chest. "Well, hello there."

"This okay?"

"I'm pretty sure it's the single most amazing experience of my life, but . . ." She clenched her inner muscles. Good thing she practiced her Kegels on a regular basis because he gave a guttural moan, his fiery gaze like a lit fuse, threatening to incinerate her into the mattress. She licked her lips and locked her ankles around his muscular ass. "Put your back into it, Cap. Oh my God. Oh my *good God.* Give me everything you got."

"Christ." His gruff laughter vibrated through her as he inclined his head, rested his forehead on hers and bore down with his hips. "You're something else."

"Yeah." She twisted, rolling over, rising up so she sat on him, ready to ride. Good lord, he was beautiful. Marvelously made and all for her taking. "Something you're making feel pretty darn amazing."

"Fuck, girl." His hands grabbed her hips, dragged her down deeper. "How is your pussy such a perfect fit?"

"I was made for you." She panted, breasts bouncing as she slammed her shoulder blades together, raised her hands to the back of her head. His smoldering gaze drenched her pussy as she rolled her hips. The sound of smacking flesh and uneven breaths filled the room.

She was getting the chance to ride Jed West, and such an event meant two things:

One: She wouldn't be able to walk straight for a week.

Two: She wanted to leave his world rocked.

Oh, hell yeah, she did. Someday, when his memories drifted to the one woman who blew his mind, ruined him for all others, she was bound and determined that it would be her name on his lips.

But despite her resolve, her attention to detail wavered. Too hard to remain focused when every inch of her body, down to a cellular level, seethed with hot, blissful fire. She struck against him, flint to his steel, flame to his kindling. Even as she rode ever harder, it became more and more obvious that he never intended to be a passive stallion. His powerful hips pumped and rolled, and at this angle he sank deeper and deeper, the sweet pierce of his cock so thickly overwhelming that it almost made her pussy quake from pain, except for the fact that it never left the side of pleasure.

He grunted, palming her breasts, her nipples puckering against the rough calluses on his palms. With an urgent jerk, he rose up, nuzzling her cleavage, sucking in her aching tips with such beautifully tortuous pulses as invisible flames began to lick at her core. She had to bite her lip to keep from screaming.

At the first sign of her inner contractions, he halted his sweet assault, grabbing her ass, his fingers squeezing in a warning. "Not yet, Vixen." He tilted back his neck, the corded muscle in his neck straining. "Not. Fucking. Yet."

She fashioned her mouth in a pout. "Why?"

"Because you're going to wait until I say so," he grated as if this was a common statement of fact, like naming the capital of Rhode Island or the second column on the periodic table. This alpha dirty talk got her in the game. Front and center. White heat scorched her spine. She took and took and took, until her skin was too sensitive, her need cutting like a blade. This feeling was going to devour her, swallow her whole. And at last, finally, she couldn't take it anymore. It was too much. Too him. Too them. Too damn perfect. She practically purred.

A surge of intense warmth filled her as he reached up with one of his big hands to cup her jaw. She jerked her chin down, took the tip of his thumb into her mouth, sucked it hard.

"Now." His groan came from deep in his throat. His eyes burned. "I want you. I want all of you." Each word was punctuated by an urgent thrust. The headboard knocked the wall.

"Don't stop," she gasped, pulsing deep between her legs. "Jed."

"That's right, tell me who's giving it to you," he ground out.

"Jed." She gasped, angling her hips. It didn't seem possible and yet, nothing had been truer in her entire life. "Jed."

"Spread those legs wider, give it all to me. You hear that sound, you hear how soaked you are?"

"Take it," she cried out. "Take everything, just don't stop."

"I'm not stopping." He circled his pelvis over her clit until she writhed. "You were made for me, made for me to fuck you good."

"Yes. The best." Her entire body went taut, the powerful muscles in his chest bunching. In another few seconds she'd snap into a million pieces, never to be put back together. "Oh God, faster. Please."

He buried himself to the root, his balls slamming the bottom of her pussy, his rhythm getting as ragged and wild as her breath. "Tonight I own this sweet pussy."

"It's yours," she gasped as he found her mouth, slanting his lips to hers. She moaned as his tongue stroked over her teeth to tangle with hers. The peak made her dizzy. She couldn't hold on. His powerful thrust gave way to uncontrolled bucking and she gave in, falling.

"That's right, take it." He strained, bearing down, filling her to the brim. His chest heaved. His jaw clenched. "Take everything I'm giving." He was at his end and she was there, ready.

Afterward, they collapsed against each other, sweat slick and panting. He opened his arms and she burrowed in, giving his pec a teasing bite, right over the heart and murmured, "That was amazing."

"No." He stared at her with wonder as his arm snaked around her waist. "*You're* what's amazing, Breezy Angel."

Chapter Twelve

SUNLIGHT WARMED JED's cheek, slowly returning him to consciousness. What the hell time was it? He never slept in. He opened his eyes and jolted. Two wide silver-blue eyes stared inches from his own.

"This a habit of yours?" he asked in a sleep-husky voice, scrubbing his face. "Early morning spying?"

"From what I've observed, you're a fascinating sleeper." Breezy grinned, rising onto one elbow. "First off, you get this little twitch right here." She pointed at a spot next to his left eye. "And second, you're a total pillow hugger."

"Hey, been a while since I've had a pretty woman to hold." He gathered her closer, breathed in her coconut oil scent. "Had to make do."

Her face went expressionless as she absorbed his statement. "See, I don't get it. You could score with most of the available women in this town. Any other guy would cash in on that sort of sexual gold mine. Get laid every night of the week. Twice on Saturday. The puck bunnies alone must be hopping after you all the time."

"It feels wrong going after a fan." He gave a one-shouldered shrug. "Too easy, like I'm taking advantage and besides, I prefer a challenge."

"Hey." She nibbled the corner of her lower lip, as if debating something. "About that . . . you know how I mentioned that my family are hockey fans?"

"Yeah." He tucked the blankets in further around them. "But I'm not sleeping with your family." He didn't want to talk about fans. Or hockey. Just them. Just be in this moment.

"Right, ha ha, funny guy." She squeezed his hand. "It's just that . . . I'd never want you to think that I was using you."

"You don't want to use me?" He raised the back of her hand to his mouth, the tip of his tongue licking between two of her fingers, a small, intimate gesture she felt all the way between her legs. "Gotta say, that's the worst news I've heard all morning. And here I was going to be a nice guy and feed you Belgian waffles in bed."

"Feeding me?" Her brow furrowed as she glanced around the room. "But you haven't—"

He stopped her with a finger to her lips. "Yet."

She nipped him. "Ready to fire up your fancy mixer?"

"Better believe it." He snuggled her closer, his gaze

losing focus as he stared at her mouth. "Hope you're hungry."

"I am, but food always tastes best when you're ravenous, right?" She hiked the sheet over their heads, the distracted look on her face fading. "Help me work up that appetite."

And after forty-five sweaty minutes, after a round of old-fashioned missionary that felt anything but, they collapsed, sated and glowing. Her belly audibly rumbled against his abs. Her eyes went wide. "Oops."

"Back in a flash, Vixen." He kissed her quick, grabbed the sweats next to his bed and yanked them on before striding out of the room with a whistle.

The grin didn't leave his face until he dropped a dollop of butter into the waffle iron, listening to the hiss and splutter. He chopped strawberries into thin slices, walked to the fridge and grabbed the carton of heavy whipping cream. The muffled sound of humming floated out from his bedroom. He grinned to himself. He hadn't known what to call the out-of-sorts, aimless feeling that had gripped him of late, but he knew the name now.

Loneliness.

He beat the cream, adding a few tablespoons of sugar. This could be the start of something big. When he first saw Breezy stumble out of the library bathroom in that ridiculous superhero suit, he had no idea that he was about to encounter the most intriguing woman he'd met . . . maybe ever.

He cocked his head. What the hell was she singing? Madonna? "Like a Virgin" Madonna? Her voice cracked hitting a high note. He chuckled as the waffles sizzled in the press. Christ. What she lacked in skills, she made up for in enthusiasm. Hell, he felt like singing too. His head felt clear. His fucking dick too. The pipes cleared out.

His phone buzzed on the counter—a Hellions news alert from *The Post*. He glanced at the headline, the article conjecturing over the chances of a lockout next season. Negotiations were breaking down at the highest levels. His heart sank when he spied the byline.

Neve Angel.

He liked Breezy's sister, enjoyed her company when they sat down for interviews or she sauntered through his locker room taking zero shit. But that was all work.

This was his life.

His stomach muscles flexed in an uneasy twitch. If things continued the way they were going, Breezy would eventually find out about Travis. It wasn't that he was ashamed of his brother's traumatic brain injury, more that he considered himself the fierce guardian of his family's privacy. He'd gone years without having anything from his private life shared, a damn near miracle.

Once Breezy knew, Neve would too.

It wasn't by any means a deal breaker, but still . . . something to consider.

Not to mention his own private fears. The fact the game he loved might not be worth sacrificing his future health.

monthly mortgage and didn't get how scary it would be to sink further into debt. Plus there was no guarantee that the neighborhood might appreciate a good quality children's bookstore. She hadn't even done a full business plan. Just had a hunch she was right.

Taking a leap in life came with a risk, a better than average chance of crashing and burning, falling to Earth like a stupid Icarus. Every time she imagined moving forward, Mom's voice piped into the back of her head. *How are you planning on paying for health insurance? What about days off? Are you going to hire staff and give them health insurance? Do you know what the failure rate for small businesses is in this city? This state? This country?*

Every question would underline and highlight the same fact.

Not. Good. Enough.

Same when Mom had been her skating coach.

"Penny for your thoughts." Jed returned her back into the present. "Where'd you go?"

"Nowhere good," she replied. "It's like I have this voice in my head. Not a crazy one telling me to go hold up a 7-Eleven or wear a tinfoil hat," she hastily tacked on. "We all have chatter going on in our minds to some degree. But whenever I stop and listen to my thoughts, more often than not, they are sort of acting like assholes."

Jed nodded once. "Sports psychology is big business, much of it devoted to tackling this very thing.

The research is clear. Athletes that commit to practicing positive self-talk see upticks in their performance. Giving in to negativity reduces success."

"You sound like a motivational video," she teased.

"I shot one of those last week," he deadpanned.

"I can't tell if you are kidding, but then, they don't let you have that *C* on your jersey for being a slouch."

"So you want to open a children's bookshop, but are afraid you aren't cut out for it?" He frowned faintly. "Why?"

"Because I love books. But I don't have the first clue about running a small business."

"You know what people are reading. Understand the market."

"But what if I fail?" Hearing him behave like this wasn't a ridiculous idea made the idea more real.

Lord knew she thought about it enough. Even knew the perfect space on a tree-lined street in the Cherry Creek neighborhood, a charming brick-and-mortar building with big bright windows and hardwood floors. It was located next to a popular coffee shop and close to a toy shop and kid's clothing store.

She even had the name picked out: Itsy Bitsy Books.

"But I don't know anything about finance," she blurted, although the business plan shoved in a binder on her bookshelf begged to differ.

"*But*. There's that word again." He crawled over her, kissing it away. "I happen to know a guy who knows a guy. And that guy got a degree in Finance from Stanford. And that guy knows how to negotiate contracts like nobody's business. Here's my secret. A few people know it, but I need you to hear it before we go any further."

Nerves bubbled in her belly even as she forced a determined smile. What could he possibly confess that made him go dark and impenetrable? Almost as if he was cloaked in shame. "Go on."

"Look. You should know, I'm not a big reader . . . I get distracted and restless. My mind starts to wander. But you, *you* live and breathe stories. They're your oxygen or something."

"It's true." She reached out and touched his perfect, square jaw. "Books are proof to me that magic really does exist in the world."

"I don't want you to think that I'm not smart," he muttered, still not making direct eye contact. "In school I was always in remedial English. My dad would give me shit."

Rage on his behalf bubbled in her belly. "I'd never think that in a million years. Honestly, I bet a reader does live inside of you. It's a matter of finding just the right book."

"You make it sound like a challenge," he said ruefully, even as the wrinkles in his brow smoothed.

She regarded him steadily. "I see a guy who needs the right story and then there will be no looking back."

"That a fact?" He peppered kisses down her neck, over her breast, to her belly and kept right on going.

"Call it professional intuition, but I'll find you a book."

"Right after I eat you like a sundae with a cherry on top."

He made good on the promise and as she came beneath his clever mouth, another voice in her head appeared. One that marched over to the negative mumbler and punched it hard, right in the nose, then grabbed it by the back of the head and forced it to bear witness to the activity below, Jed West going to town on her pussy like a champ.

What was she even thinking about? This was like a perverted remake of *Inside Out*.

She crashed her head back in the pillow and covered her face with her hands to muffle a giggle.

"This funny, is it?" He stuck a finger inside her and pushed right in the spot that sent her back arching.

"I'm happy," she gasped. Because for once, it was as if everything was possible, like maybe all her dreams really could come true.

Chapter Thirteen

JED PRETENDED TO watch the TiVo'd Denver Nuggets game from last night, but spent more time glancing over at Breezy who sat, feet propped in his lap, wearing nothing but one of his old college jerseys, frowning into space.

"Okay, so what was your favorite childhood story?" she asked at last. "Not counting *The Giving Tree*." Her joking tone belied the serious expression on her face, guess she meant what she said, about finding the magical book that would get him excited about reading.

"Okay, okay. Hang on." He thought it over. "There was this one, it was weird and I don't remember the name, about a little boy who dreams he is in a baker's kitchen. There's this whole bit about how he was in the milk, and the milk was in him." He laughed, embarrassed. "I don't know how to explain it, it sounds stupid when I try to—"

"*In The Night Kitchen*!" She clapped her hands. "An interesting choice. More surreal then I would have pegged for you. Fascinating."

"Oh yeah?" He tweaked one of her red-painted toes. "I fascinate you?" The bold vixen color killing him in the best kind of ways. He loved her big hair, her soft body, her polished nails. She was womanly, sexy, and yet . . . if she was going to probe him, take him out of his comfort zone—it could go both ways.

"You definitely do." She nodded solemnly.

"Okay, okay, so you want to inspire the jock to read, I get it. But what about you?" He rubbed her feet, pressing hard on her arches.

"Mmm. That's good." Her eyes rolled a little, her lips parting as his massage deepened. "What about me?"

"You're pushing me out of my comfort zones. How about you? What sports do you play?"

"Oh. Uh. Hmm." Her lids flew open and she regarded him wide-eyed. "Does stocking shelves count?"

A chuckle rumbled through him. "Not letting you get off so easily."

"I used to ice skate," she said with a shrug.

"You skated?" That surprised him. In a good way.

Until her snub nose wrinkled.

"Honestly? I hated it. I mean, I love watching people skate, but my own legs and feet? They just don't work that way. Neve was pretty good at it, way better than me. My mom coached us. I think she was hoping for more, but I let her down the most." She shrugged with a grin. "What can I say? I'm a total klutz."

Her lighthearted tone didn't mask the flash of pain in her eyes.

"Breezy Angel." He stared at her a long minute and then checked his watch. "I never thought I'd say this to you in a million years, but go put some pants on."

"What are you talking about?" She sat back, drawing in her knees, giving him the briefest flash of her near perfect pink pussy. "Why?"

His mouth watered. He could forget everything, just wrap those sweet thighs around his neck, and lose himself in her.

But, fuck. No. He took a steadying breath. This was important, because she hadn't just found her way into his pants, but also his heart.

Fifteen minutes later they were on the road, in his Land Rover. She was being a good sport despite the fact he hadn't offered up a single detail of his plan. Her hair twisted into one of her high knots, a few wild tendrils escaping to brush the side of her neck, right at the place where her pulse fluttered—the only clue that she wasn't as relaxed as she might seem.

When he exited onto the off-ramp, her hands dropped to her lap. Her head jerked as if wanting to glance over in his direction, but she didn't allow it.

"We're here," he said, parking in an empty space, reaching for his Hellions ball cap.

"Hoo boy. I was afraid you might be taking me here," she said flatly, eyeing the sign on the building. "Mile High Skate Center. This is where Mom used to give me lessons."

"I figured as much. Most kids in the city do them here."

"Just tell me straight." She took off her sunglasses and ducked her chin. "Is it funny to you? I'm not kidding. I really do suck. And if you want to laugh then there are easier ways to—"

"Vixen." He reached and cupped her chin, turning her face toward his. "It's like what you said with the books."

Her brows mashed. "I don't get it."

"You believe there is a reader inside me, just waiting to get out. It's a question of finding the right story, the one that excites me, right?"

She nodded, confusion still plain on her face.

"Well it's the same here with this. I think there is a skater inside you, but you need the right teacher."

GOOD LORD, MILE High even smelled the same, the damp rubber tickling her nose, the chemicals in the ice, the cold pizza from a birthday party set up in the corner. It was open skate time and zippy pop music pulsed over the speakers as kids flew past, and couples hand in hand.

While she got fitted for skates, Jed signed a quick autograph for a teenage girl behind the counter, one who clutched the scrap of paper he'd touched as if she'd sleep with it tonight, treasure his scrawled signature for all time.

Breezy had to smile, even as her fingers trembled while she tightened her laces. It hadn't been all that long since she'd been the same way. And yet here she was, about to step into her worst nightmare, simply because Jed asked, because he believed he could make her enjoy this.

He was already laced up by the time she finished.

"This is ridiculous," she muttered, hobbling toward him, ankles awkward. "Jed West at a kiddie open skate?"

He shrugged. "I like it. In fact, a couple of times during the year I come alone."

"You're lying to make me feel better."

He took her hand, steadying her balance with a gentle squeeze. "One thing I won't do is lie to you, Vixen. I started skating because it was so much goddamn fun. Coming here? It helps remind me of that part of it. Gets me out of my head. Loosens me up."

They reached the ice. If she closed her eyes, she'd still be able to hear her mom screaming at her from the side. *Focus!*

"Ready?" He stepped out and gave her a gentle tug. "Keep your head steady and if you start to wobble, fix your gaze on a point in the distance."

"Fair warning." She licked her lips, joining him. "I'm going to make a total fool out of myself."

True to her word, she slipped immediately, but he caught her by the waist, keeping her steady. "First rule is stay loose. You don't want to be tense out here."

"Easier said than done." Any second she was going to do the splits.

"What's the worst that can happen?" he asked her, and just like that he was sprawled, ass smacking the ice, his long legs akimbo at awkward angles.

Breezy clasped a hand over her mouth, a few families openly pointing. "What are you doing?"

"Falling!" His smile lit his own face. "That's the worst thing that can happen, and guess what, it's not so bad."

She laughed in spite of herself as the truth settled on her. "I guess you're right." Her mom had made it seem like that, but Jed had a point. And the tender way he watched her, if she fell, it might actually feel like flying.

Chapter Fourteen

———————————————————

BREEZY STRODE THROUGH the front door of the library and every head in the place swiveled in her direction. She felt as if she starred in her own personal musical and this was the part where she leaped onto the reference desk to belt out a solo. She just spent the past three days having the best time of her life with the best man she'd ever know.

Seriously. Everyone really was looking at her. Two women even pointed.

Had word gotten out that she'd been shacking up with Jed West? Maybe someone saw them at the rink. Her heart raced. Because he wasn't Jed West anymore. Or Westy. Or even a hockey god. Not to her—he was just Jed. The guy she was falling head over heels for. The man who made her waffles in bed and went down on her not as a cursory to-do item before getting his rocks off but treated it like a hobby, an artistic craft that he was determined to put ten thousand hours in to become a master.

"Breezy!" A volunteer waved.

She waved back but kept going. A little faster. She wasn't ready to talk about this weekend. As wonderful as it was, as much as she wanted to sing it from the rooftops, she wasn't sure what to say. She didn't want to name what was happening because it was too new. Too fragile. If she looked at it too hard it might pop like a frigging soap bubble.

When she was with him it felt so real, so natural, so right. But away. Doubt settled in. That little mumbling voice had put ice on its broken nose and was piping back up.

When she got up to her desk, she hadn't put down her bag before Daisy ran in.

"Want the bad news, or worse news first?" Her assistant sounded out of breath.

Not how anyone wants to start out the week. "Bad?"

"You have a giant piece of chocolate-glazed donut stuck to your top lip. Either that or you need to see a dermatologist like right now because that's one funky-looking mole."

"What?" Breezy reached up and *crap*. Sure enough the glazed donut she'd bought on the way over was affixed to her face. She'd walked through the entire library covered in her breakfast. No wonder there were pointers! What could be worse than that?

"Also, Tater Tots called a meeting." Daisy sounded worried. "Just for the children's department. You. Me. Her."

"Maybe she wants to give us raises." Breezy tried to laugh, but it wasn't funny. In fact, her stomach dropped a few inches and a cool chill slithered across her lower back.

"Not likely. She was wearing red shoes today." Daisy crossed her arms. "You know what that means."

"Her butt-kickers." Tater Tots had a pair of fire-engine red pumps and was fond of saying she wore them when she wanted to kick ass and take names.

Daisy turned around and stuck out her booty. "Mine is bony. This is going to hurt."

Breezy giggled despite herself. "I'll sacrifice myself for you, okay? My butt can take a lickin' and keep on tickin'."

"What will happen if we get fired? I need this job. My student loans are killing me. Plus my home life isn't good." Unexpected tears sheened her eyes. "Not good at all. My husband hasn't been able to find work for months. If I can't keep this position, there goes our apartment, our health care . . . everything."

"No one is losing their job." Breezy opened up her purse and pulled out her own secret weapon. Lady Dracula. Her boldest, reddest lipstick. If Tater Tots wanted to threaten her department, she wouldn't go without a fight.

JED'S DOCTOR APPOINTMENT turned into a full morning at the hospital, going through a battery of tests. First a full neurological examination that checked his vision, hearing, reflexes, strength and coordination, then cognitive ones to test his recall, concentration and memory. Finally he went and did an MRI.

In the end, his fears were confirmed.

Diagnosis: concussion.

"How long will the symptoms persist?" he asked the doctor.

"All brain injuries are different," the neurologist said carefully. "And that means there's no one-size-fits-all when it comes to recovery."

"Translate that into practical English, Doc." Jed scrubbed his brow and sat back, dazed, arms tight across against his chest. "You know, for my career, my entire damn life?"

The doctor took off his glasses and went silent. "The damage that I am seeing here isn't going to sink you," he said at last. "But there's a cumulative impact that worries me."

It was a hell of a thing, experiencing a long-dreaded moment in all its gut-twisting anxiety. He exhaled a long ragged breath, a little detached from his body, as if viewing himself from a distance, his heartbeat steady but heavy, the reverberations shuddering against his chest.

The air-conditioning hummed even as the room felt oppressively overwarm. Darkness loomed but he shoved it back, squaring his shoulders. Now that the worst had happened, he didn't have to fear it. Not anymore.

"Don't get me wrong," the doctor said with a sheepish chuckle. "I'm one hell of a Hellions fan, and would hate to see you leave the game." The smile faded from his face. "But I see a lot of athletes sitting where you sit now who have to make a choice. Continue with the game, spin the roulette wheel, play the odds and risk long-term, permanent, irreversible brain damage. Or walk away."

Jed cleared his throat, coughed once in his fist and swallowed, swallowing again. But nothing was going to budge the knot choking his throat. "Guess I should be glad to get the option, Doc." Because many times— too fucking many—an athlete didn't get the luxury of making this kind of shitty decision. An athlete like his brother, Travis, a guy just entering manhood who had big dreams, who went hard, had a champion's heart pumping in his chest.

Jed raked a hand through his hair, fist tugging the strands at the root.

Travis was a player who didn't know how to give up. Didn't quit. Didn't know that his brain was a ticking time bomb.

"You ever give thought to life beyond hockey?" the doctor asked.

Jed shrugged. Hard to admit the truth, but not really. When Breezy had told him of her uncertainties about opening a children's bookshop, he'd been a hypocrite of the highest order, spouting off all that motivational "Rah! Rah! Go team!" crap.

The truth was that he didn't know what to do after leaving hockey. He didn't have the first fucking clue.

He punched a number into his phone as he left the hospital, the one he never called enough.

"Hello?" His sister-in-law, Tamara's, voice was threadbare. In high school, she'd been the vivacious captain of the color guard and reigned alongside Travis as king and queen of the high school. She'd gotten pregnant during Travis's second year at UCLA, but his brother had done the right thing and put a ring on his girl's finger.

That had been the kind of guy he was.

Everyone had been happy. Even their conservative, uptight parents knew it was a good match, hasty, but inevitable. Nothing shotgun about it. The two of them had been so damn happy.

Until the accident.

"Hey, TamTam," Jed said in a low voice. "It's me."

Silence. "Been a while, Jed."

He knew enough about women to know when they said your name like that, they were pissed as hell. He didn't blame his sister-in-law. He had kept a distance, at first bewildered and not sure what to do. As his brother recovered from the brain injury, gaining limited capacity, it became sadly evident that Travis was never going to be Travis again. In his place rose up a sad man, angry, depressed and the last person he wanted to see was his younger brother who still had a bright career waiting for him. Different sport, but an athlete is an athlete is an athlete.

"I'm sorry. He's having one of his bad days," Tamara said slowly.

She tended to downplay his brother's outbursts so this frank admission didn't bode well.

"How can I help?"

Tamara's sigh sounded as if it came from the bottom of her feet. "There's nothing anybody can do."

Uncomfortable silence filled the airwaves.

"Did you get the stack of books that I sent Josh?" Talking about his nephew might cheer her up. Her only son was a bright light in a too-often dark life.

"He loved them." Her voice softened. "Especially the Percy Jackson one. Sorry I didn't have him call to say thank you . . . there's just been a lot going on." Her voice dropped into a whisper. "Josh is staying at my parents' house right now. Just while . . ." She trailed off. "Jed? Hang on a second, Travis just walked into the kitchen. I'll—uh—I'll see if he wants to say hello."

Tam must have covered the phone. The words muffled, then, "Hey, brother. Long time no talk."

"Travis." Jed stiffened, recalibrating. His brother hated to talk to him. He hadn't wanted to speak to him for a couple of years. "Hey, man."

"Those were some hard-fought playoffs, huh?" His brother's deep voice was familiar, even though he sounded like a stranger. "I watched, you know. Game seven. Dad came over."

"Yeah, Detroit was a strong opponent."

"Hell of a hit you took."

"Yeah. About that." Jed cleared his throat, debating a moment. He didn't do personal conversations with his brother anymore. Travis never wanted to go there. But the guilt was there, as it always was when they spoke, pressing on all sides. The silent question pulsing through his brain.

Why you?

Why not me?

"I've been having some issues since the playoffs." Jed coughed once into his fist. "Double vision. Headaches. Saw a doctor and they're saying I should give it up."

There was a beat of silence before his brother laughed. "You're shitting me."

"Not at all." He raked a hand through his hair. "I'm probably going to retire."

There it was. The words were finally spoken out loud.

"Get out before what, you're a fuckup like me?" Travis's words took on a bite. "That's great. Real great. Tell you what though. While the rest of the world thinks of you as some sort of big hero, I know the truth. The real Jed West is a piece of shit who abandoned his brother." His voice rose in volume. "Left his sister-in-law and only nephew financially without help and living hand-to-mouth."

"What are you talking about?" Jed's back stiffened, steel in his spine. "I have money deposited into your account every month. If it's not enough, I didn't know, no one ever told me."

But should they have had to? Tam was proud, not the type to come to him hat in hand.

"Do me a solid and admit the truth," Travis continued as if he hadn't spoken. "Admit that you don't think about us. That we aren't big winners and therefore not worth your time. Because big deal Jed West only surrounds himself with successes. I get it. I remember how it went in our house, but—"

"I hate asking this, man, but give it to me straight." Jed's gut was a knot. Substance abuse added fuel to the fire of Travis's injury. Objectively, he knew his brother's front lobe injury caused ugly thoughts and addictive behavior. But it was another thing to be on the wrong end of one of his binges. "Are you drinking?"

Christ, Tam had done the right thing getting her son out of the home. Josh didn't need to be around this. "Do you need me to fly out there because I can be on a plane tonight, scratch that, I can be on one in a few hours."

There was a click and exhale. What the hell? Was his brother smoking too?

"Why did you call?" Travis's voice slurred.

Jed paused, maybe honesty would help build a bridge, break through what felt like insurmountable barriers. "Like I said. I've been thinking about my life. What I'm doing. Made me think of you too."

"Gotcha." Another exhale. "Guess it wasn't enough you tried to be like me growing up." Travis gave a hoarse bitter laugh. "Now you're still trying to follow in your big bro's footsteps. Make sure you tell Dad. He'll be so fucking proud. Both of his boys. Both winners."

"Travis, baby," Tamara pleaded in the background. "Put down the phone. Come inside and I'll fix you something to eat."

"Don't call here anymore." Travis slammed down the phone so hard that Jed's ear rang.

It didn't take long for Tamara to give him a follow-up text: *I asked your mom to email you an update. It's too hard to talk when he is in these moods.*

Jed sank back into his chair, refreshing his inbox until at last Mom's email popped in. Looked like one of her infrequent, short and to-the-point updates. One that managed to say everything and nothing at all.

Subject: Travis

Message: Hope this note finds you well. Your brother is being moved from his home to a long-term care facility. In addition to his chronic irritability and aggression, he is now demonstrating worrying signs of mania. His spending habits are out of control and he was arrested yesterday for aggravated assault outside their local grocery store. It is likely CTE but

as the doctors told us, the condition is impossible to
diagnose at this time.

> *Best*
> *Mom*

"Ah shit." He tossed his phone onto the car seat and buried his face in his hands. "Shit. Shit. Shit."

CTE, or chronic brain encephalopathy, couldn't be diagnosed outside of an autopsy, but the hallmark symptoms were memory loss, confusion, impaired judgment, aggression and the depressing laundry list went on and on.

Jed had one guess where the money had gone that he'd been sending. Nowhere good. Travis must have spent it. But, shit. A dull pain throbbed in his temples as he rubbed his forehead. His big brother was still his big brother. Would always be his brother. But there was no doubt that the man he was, the man he should be now, was gone forever, a stranger.

And even after all this time, that fact still made his stomach turn.

After his brother's injury, his parents had faded away. They still got together for Christmas once in a while. But they seemed to have wrapped themselves in some sort of shield. Maybe unable to bear seeing Jed or be happy for his success because of the guilt over what their other—favorite—son had had and lost.

And maybe Jed never quite forgave their dad for riding his sons' asses, demanding nothing but the best.

Bile rose in Jed's throat. He was good at keeping these shitty feelings on lockdown. Too good.

He started driving and his turns weren't aimless. He was going to the library. He needed to see Breezy. To see her smile. Hear her laugh. Because she'd settle him. It's what she did. He could want her too. Lose himself in her beautiful body all over again afterward while she sang funny little songs under her breath or confessed sweet dreams like opening a children's bookstore.

He pulled into the Rosedale Branch Library and didn't even get out of his car. Because there was Breezy coming through the front door, looking like someone had drowned her pet kitten.

She stopped short upon seeing him.

"You can't be here," she said stiffly.

"No?" He froze, unsure.

"Because if I see you right now, I'm going to cry, and I swore. I swore I wasn't going to cry."

"What's happened?"

"Nothing except for the fact you are looking at the former head of the children's department."

"You lost your job?"

"Lost? No. I wouldn't say that." Breezy's nose was red and her eyes glistening with unshed tears. "It was taken away."

The wobble in her lower lip threatened to undo him.

"She said the decision wasn't personal. My boss. Tater Tots." She reached up and dabbed her nose. "But got to say, it felt pretty darn personal to me. In fact, the witch couldn't stop smiling the whole time she talked about how we were being merged with the Oak Ridge children's library. In fact she said that I should be happy, because this change meant that the rest of Rosedale could remain operational and I didn't want that, didn't I?" She dug the heels of her hands into her eyes. "And I don't. But I want a job!"

"Tell you what. I'm gonna drive you home." He took her hand and led her toward the parking lot. "We can come back and get your car later." Once she was buckled inside his Land Rover, he took off for Breezy's cottage. She didn't respond, just gazed out the passenger window. Outside the sun was shining, people were jogging, walking their dogs, talking on their phones. He reached over and took her hand. "It's a hell of a thing to have your world turned upside down when no one else has the first fucking clue."

How good would it feel to continue on, tell her how much he understood the feelings that must be roiling inside her, but that wouldn't be fair. This was her moment to grieve. And he didn't want to pull the rug out to make it about him too.

"If you don't keep your eyes on the road, Cap, we are going to end up in someone's flower patch." Breezy squeezed his hand in a gesture of quiet thank-you.

"Maybe losing your job will turn out to be an opportunity. Everything doesn't have to be lost, you know?" He parked in front of her house, smiling when he got out and she waited for him. After he opened the door, he continued, "What if this is the push that you needed to open Itsy Bitsy?"

"Maybe." She furrowed her brow and shrugged.

"I think you're right." He reached down and scooped her up cradling her against him as she shrieked with surprised laughter. "But right now I'm going to fly you into that house, Vixen, and turn this bad day around."

When it came to his family, or even his own body, he was failing. But with her—right now—he could pretend to be the superhero the rest of the world believed him to be.

Chapter Fifteen

SHE SANK DOWN into the tub, the vanilla-scented suds piling up to her chin, the hot water relaxing her tense muscles. As soon as they got into the house, Jed ordered her to strip. Before she could even get excited, he declared that he was drawing her a bath, that a day like today qualified for a good long soak.

And while she wanted nothing more than his hands on her, have his clever mouth and devastating tongue driving away the memories of the terrible day, she couldn't ignore the fact that she was so wound up that she might split into two before he took her over the edge.

Three candles flickered on the edge of the tub, mirroring a similar flicker inside her.

Hope.

She'd never had anyone pamper her like this; at his best, Rory had once bought her a gas station rose.

She wanted to hug the old version of herself who had no idea it could be better, or that she deserved more. That she deserved a real man who would tend to her needs not because he wanted to get something in return, but because he simply wanted to put a smile on her face.

As she began to unwind, the memory of her firing crept in. No point in even trying to hold it back, might as well feel all the things, let the poison out and move on.

Tater Tots had called Breezy and Daisy into her office. As soon as she'd walked inside, Breezy had known what was coming. Her boss was seated, hands resolutely crossed and placed in the center of the desk, her lips angled down a slight jowly frown, resembling Donald Trump from his days hosting *The Apprentice*. She started out highlighting the budget woes, the funding cuts, gaining speed as it became clear the children's department was going to close, other branches would increase their programming.

"During these tough times, we must make tough decisions. Not to worry, you'll land on your feet," Tater Tots had said, wrapping up a short "you're fired" speech, before turning to Daisy. "One staff member was allowed to transfer to the adult desk. A difficult decision to be sure."

Yeah. Sure. Breezy had silently absorbed the impact while all the while the scream, "But I have seniority," danced on the tip of her tongue. Not to mention the fact that she'd built up the department.

"Thank you, Janet." Daisy hadn't looked over at her old boss.

"When is this termination effective?" Breezy had asked. So many thoughts had rolled through her mind, how to say goodbye to the volunteers, to the neighborhood families, to the place that she had known since she graduated university—this had been her first "real" job. Her only job.

"Effective immediately. Easier that way."

"I'm sorry, Boss." Daisy had begun to sniffle. "I haven't talked about this, but Dan is leaving. His unemployment got to him and he isn't coping. I have the two kids, I have to be able to support us."

It was only then that Breezy had blown the cobwebs from her eyes, seen how haggard her assistant looked. Tiny pimples pebbled her forehead while bags drooped under her eyes.

How could Breezy begrudge this promotional opportunity for her faithful assistant? She had a mortgage, but she wasn't a single mom with two kids.

"I'm happy for you." She'd forced a smile. "Really happy. You deserve all the good things to happen to you."

And with that she stood up and dusted off her thighs. "As for you, *Janet*." God, she'd sounded like Newman on *Seinfeld* when he said "Jerry." "I worked my butt off here and I did a damn good job. I understand that sometimes it's easy to want to keep the status quo and I wish you the best right here. Meanwhile I'm off to start living my best life, using my talents and creativity."

It felt good to say those words, so much so that it didn't—hardly—matter when she'd tripped leaving her former boss's office. It wasn't until she got to her desk rummaging around for a box to store her precious items, that the tears threatened. It was one thing to talk tough, another entirely to *be* tough.

The desire to be brave and take risks welled inside her, but that didn't cancel out that this was a humongous life change, one that felt particularly overwhelming when she had just bought her first-ever house.

And she wasn't going to go beg for her mother's help to bail her out of this financial hole. Uh-uh, no way. No how. Besides she was talking about taking a trip to the Winter Olympics and needed to save. She just wanted a friendly ear, or rather, one friendly ear in particular.

Jed's.

The bathroom door cracked and he entered carrying a full wineglass and—bless him—the rest of the bottle. "Penny for your thoughts?" He knelt down and handed her the glass and smoothed back some hair stuck to her forehead.

"I love this house," she said, reaching out to touch a damp tile, slick with the room's steam. "But I've gotten over my head. I still have a hole in my bedroom ceiling, a roof that probably needs replacing and no job to pay any mortgage." She started to giggle and when she started she couldn't stop. Who knew staring into the black abyss could be so funny, in a "we're all going to die" way?

He frowned. "You going off the deep end, Vixen?"

"No, but how much can you get for plasma these

days? Oh! And there's always those egg ads in the free newspapers around town. Or I guess I could sell my body?" she quipped.

"To another man?" His gaze burned with palpable possession. "I'm gonna stop you right there." He ripped off his T-shirt; his belt, boxers and jeans followed in quick succession. Straightening, he stood naked, all carved muscle and perfect bone structure, and stepped into her bath.

"You getting dirty?"

"Filthy." He didn't smile. Instead his hand, slippery with bubble soap, slid up her thigh, the pad of his thick fingers tracing the seam of her inner lips with slow steady strokes. "Feel this? This right here?"

"Yes." She gasped.

He slid in one big finger, crooking it. Her hand flew to the edge of the tub, gripping the cool ceramic. "This is me, making your pussy mine." His words had an intense growl, even as humor flared in his eyes. "I'll help look after you, Breezy."

"Will you?" Her lids lowered. "Even if I do this?" She grabbed his cock at the root, it was already stiff in her hand. "Because two can play at this game."

"You got me." His eyes gleamed. "What are you going to do with me?"

She gave him a sassy push, taking her hair and twisting the coil into a quick messy bun.

It wasn't until she parted his muscular thighs that it

seemed to dawn on him what she was about to do. And his cock reacted, rising out of the water.

"Confession." She had goose bumps despite the water's temperature. "I'm not a pro at this."

"Got to say, anything you're gonna try will be pretty damn good." His voice dropped an octave, raspy and brimming with need.

She let her lips part over his gleaming tip, relaxing a little. So far so good. This didn't feel scary, it felt good. Powerful even. The sexiest, most self-assured man that she'd ever known was sucking in his slab of strong abdominal muscles and hissing with pleasure, all because of her. Emboldened, she took hold of him around the base and let him slide the way down to her throat. Coming back up she nicked him with her top teeth. "My God, sorry," she yelped.

He opened one eye. "Do I look sorry?" He sounded hoarse. "More."

She returned to her work, letting him slide up and down her tongue, practicing switching up the pressure, what it was like to hollow her cheeks, to stroke the thick rigid vein along the shaft with the flat of her tongue, to suck the tip like a lollipop, to reach under and cup the soft, slick sac in her hand.

His appreciative moan sent a pulse through her pussy before he reached out and gently fisted her knot of hair. "Let me inside you."

"I've never done this." She shook her head. "Want to keep going."

His lids grew heavy. A muscle twitched in his temple. "You've never done what?"

"Had a guy . . . you know . . ." She wiped a bubble off her cheek, let the pause speak for itself.

"You're telling me that no one's ever come inside that pretty mouth?" He nearly growled the words.

"Nope. But you can role-play Neil Armstrong." She cocked a teasing brow. "If that's your kink."

He arched as she bent back, a splash of bathwater dousing one of the candles. For a moment, it almost extinguished her nerves too. But she had spoken the truth, the whole truth and nothing but the truth. She *had* wanted to do this. At least to try.

And when it happened, the hot dizzy rush, she was swept away too. Glancing up as he spent himself, their gazes locked, his own flaming with wordless marvel. When he could finally speak he shook his head. "You fooled me good."

She took a demure sip of wine. "How so?"

"I almost believed you. That it was your first time."

"I was telling the truth."

His pupils dilated. "Bullshit."

She dropped the wash cloth she was rubbing against her neck and raised a hand. "On my honor. I've never swallowed."

"Christ." He rubbed his forehead. "I've never gotten head like that in my life."

"You want to tell me about all the girls?"

"Shit. Sorry, no. I'm just saying you've got raw talent. A natural gift."

"I'm not sure you should hint to a girl that she could turn pro with her blow jobs."

"Fuck." He hooked a hand around the back of his neck. "I'm blowing this hard." His eyes opened wider. "Shit, that came out wrong. I meant to say . . ."

"I get it, I'm teasing." She giggled. "And thank you. Being told you are a sexual goddess isn't exactly a hardship. And imagine, if that was my first time, how good I can get."

"I want to own you."

"Can you afford me?" As their lips touched, electricity jumped down her spine. She wasn't talking about money, but commitment. If he wanted her for more than a fling, it was going to come at a price.

The cost of her heart.

Soft jazz music drifted from the open door and he was hard again, his shaft rigid against her thigh.

He swallowed a growl. "Let's get out and grab a condom. I want to have my way with you."

"We're good. I'm on the pill." She slid down, opening her thighs so that his tip rested at her entrance. Pinpricks tingled over her arms.

"You sure?" His lips skated over her shoulder as he pressed in, not enough to enter, but to show he meant business.

"You heard me." She traced a nail down his chest, digging ever so slightly into his rock-hard pectoral muscle. "And if you don't quit being a gentleman, then I do declare that I'm going to stop being a lady."

"Lean closer."

She bit her lip, intrigued by the mystery, only to have him suck in the lobe of her ear, a part of her so sensitive that she cried out.

"Better. That leveled the playing field some," he rasped. "So for the last time, you want me? All of me? Raw and in you?"

"That's a little like asking if I want Easter, Halloween, Thanksgiving, Christmas and the Fourth of July all at once." The idea of having him, bare-skinned and inside her, was so intimate that she nearly moaned out loud.

"All right then." He gripped her hips. "Careful what you wish for."

JESUS. HIS BRAIN stuttered while his vision went dark around the edges. He'd been inside Breezy before, lots of times now, and knew how fucking good it was in there. How tight. How hot. But this was different, and it wasn't just the fact that he was bare. This was next-level connection. He disappeared inside her inch by slow inch, losing his goddamn mind while at the exact same time finding a whole new part of himself that he didn't know existed. Deeper he went. And deeper still. With Breezy, there was always more to be discovered. Nothing was enough. He wanted in. Deeper and deeper. Until, God. Jesus, fuck. He was as far as he could get.

And he was in. All in. On every fucking thing where this woman was concerned.

This wasn't the time, when he was buried to the hilt, to tell her he was falling for her. She'd think it was the sex talking. But the truth was that he felt his heart in his throat, and it was authentic and not a line, or some sort of sex-drenched garble. It was pure. And—

"You gonna keep staring or get to it and fuck me?"

She had a filthy mouth and he loved that too.

"God, Jed." Her throat was rosy and her lips parted, reaching beneath, her fingers brushed his sac with featherlight strokes.

"You feel gorgeous, dirty girl." That was an easier truth to get out than any midfuck *L* word. "I love being inside you."

She smiled ever so slightly at that, then clenched him harder, milking his shaft, threatening to send him over the edge far earlier than he intended.

"Your pussy is so tight. I'm filling it the fuck up." He drove into her like the world was ending, like this was the last time he'd ever be inside her. Ravishing. Dominating. Water splashed onto the tile. One of the candles flicked out.

And all the while he stared directly into her beautiful face. He could barely blink, let alone look away. Swear to God, he had a window into her very soul.

Everything he gave she took and returned tenfold. The air was thick with steam and a charged electric energy. Water splashed onto the tile. Her whimpers were soft, punctuated by short sharp gasps. He'd never wanted anything so bad in his whole goddamn life.

"Breezy." He growled her name, a two-syllable command. "Breezy, you come now." And she fell apart on cue, the silky heat of orgasm rippling over the length of his cock. Because she finished, he was there too. With a possessive moan, she gripped his ass, holding him down as he lost himself in a single intense rush.

After, they didn't speak, they didn't move a single muscle, just held each other quiet in the water.

At last he stirred, but even then they didn't speak. He wasn't sure what to say. Because this felt so big and life-changing that words didn't seem up for the task. They drained the water from the tub and toweled off wordlessly. Breezy picked up the bottle of wine and took a long pull right from the bottle.

"Sorry." She dabbed her mouth. "I really needed that."

"Me too." It was time. He had to tell her what was going on with him. What he'd been putting off. "So, we got to talk."

That got her undivided attention. She lowered the bottle, dabbing her bottom lip. "What's going on?"

"I went to the doctor today. Neurologist. I've been having intermittent blurry vision since taking a big hit in game seven and . . ."

There. He'd done it. Poured out the shit he'd been

holding in. Also mentioned Travis, what had happened to him with football and his recent transfer to a long-term care facility.

"My symptoms have gotten better," he said in conclusion. "But the idea of another season? The risk doesn't seem worth it. Not when I look at my brother and everything he's lost."

"You have so much talent." She wrapped him in a hug. "You'll figure out the right path."

"You'd like me even without the *C* on my jersey?" He kept a light, joking tone, but a part of him was dead serious.

"I'd like you in a paper bag, Jed West." And when she kissed him, he knew she meant it.

Chapter Sixteen

FOR THE NEXT forty-eight hours, Breezy and Jed cocooned away from the world. They made love at his place, ordered takeout and finally drove to her cottage so she could change clothes before having an eighties movie marathon under a giant blanket fort in her living room.

Breezy had trolled her shelves, considering a few books for Jed, titles ranging from John Steinbeck to Stephen King, but dismissed them all out of hand. "None of these are right," she said, finishing up a late lunch of peanut butter and jelly sandwiches. "I feel like you need something more—"

A loud knock sounded on the front door.

They exchanged puzzled glances.

"I'm not expecting anyone." Breezy furrowed her brow. "What are the odds that is a magically delivered pizza?" Grabbing a pink fuzzy bathrobe she'd ditched under the coffee table, she knotted the ties together, making sure the neck was pulled closed. No point flashing her mystery caller.

"While you figure that out, I'm going to go make us more coffee." He crawled out and padded to the kitchen.

"Sounds good. I really need one of those No Soliciting signs."

The short, balding guy on her front step wasn't carrying a pizza. She'd never seen him before in her life.

Maybe his car had broken down?

"You Breezy Angel?" he asked, whipping out a handkerchief to dab it on his balding head. It was hot out here today. The gap between storms had left the air thick and uncharacteristically humid.

"Murphy Hallman, from the Associated Press. I have a few questions."

Her hand flew to the neck of her bathrobe. Good, no escaped boobs. "Is this about the library branch merger because I don't have any comments. Well actually I do, but nothing fit to print."

"Library merger?" The reporter frowned. "No, I'm here about Jed West. Can you make any comments on reports that he plans to retire from the game due to a head injury?"

"Jed? West?" Her voice came out high and tight. How did this reporter know she knew him?

"Shut the door." Jed's icy command came from the hall, freezing her whole body.

"Wait a second." The reporter swiveled his head. "Is he in there?" He raised his voice. "Westy, can you give a comment on—"

Jed emerged from the hall, grim-faced, and slammed the front door in the reporter's face.

"What the fuck is going on?" He stared ahead, unseeing.

She wasn't sure if the question was directed at her, or himself, or the guy on the opposite side. He glanced down to her. "How did he know I was here?"

She shrugged. "I was wondering the same thing."

It took her a second to realize that he was making a careful study of her face.

"I'm serious," she said, bristling. "It's not like I'm posting status updates about you on Facebook. If you don't believe me you're welcome to take a look. I think my last post was some random Buzzfeed article on the 100 Books to Read On A Desert Island."

"It's okay, I believe you." He peered through her curtains. "But he's not leaving. I got to make a few calls. My agent. Coach."

The illusion of a cocoon faded. He went into her room and she heard him speaking in low, measured tones. She sank onto her couch and turned on her phone, stomach fluttery with nerves. Nerves that stomped around her insides like elephants once the notifications exploded on her screen. At least a dozen were from Neve, in varying stages of alarm. She had thirty-nine messages on Facebook. What the hell? Her barely used Twitter account had two hundred and three mentions.

A car pulled up. Then another. Doors slamming. By the time Jed returned to the living room four people were milling at the edge of her front yard. A news camera was being set up. Across the street, neighbors stood, slack jawed, on their front porches, probably wondering if she was a serial killer.

Some introduction to the neighborhood.

"Yeah, of course I checked online," Jed said into his phone. "This is all over the goddamn internet. No, I'll be fine. You don't need to come down here. Okay. I see your point. Audra said the same thing, but fuck." He made a fist and punched his leg. "I wanted to control this, Coach. My decision. My rules. My timeline." He went silent, nodding at whoever was talking. "Sounds good, see you soon."

He hung up and didn't move. A small muscle twitching in his jaw was the only sign that anything was amiss.

"Was that Tor?" She knew Jed was close to the Hellions head coach but hadn't met him yet. "Is he—"

"Breezy." His voice was soft, but his eyes were dark. "You have a calendar of me in a box in the corner of your room. Care to explain?"

She wasn't afraid, per se. But good lord, he was intimidating. If this is how it felt to go up against him on the ice, she was surprised people didn't flee, skating as fast as they could in the opposite direction.

The bottom dropped out of her stomach.

While she was holed up at Jed's place, Daisy had stopped by and dropped off the box she'd forgotten at her old library desk. Of course, there had been the Jed West calendar. Not to mention her beloved coffee cup.

"Um." The truth pressed on all sides, smashing her like a shit sandwich. "Yes."

"You had a calendar and coffee cup of *me?*"

"All from before I knew you." Her words fell over themselves. "Just a little joke. At work, they knew I was a hockey fan and so for Christmas presents that is the kind of thing I got . . ."

"*You're* a hockey fan." A muscle she'd never seen before ticked right where his lower jaw hinged to the upper one.

"I mean, like I said before, my whole family is—"

"You conveniently left yourself out of that equation," he said tonelessly.

She swallowed hard, because he wasn't wrong, but she didn't have the first clue how to make her omission less creepy. "I don't know what to do," she whispered.

"You look confused." His eyes glittered. A muscle ticked in his jaw. "I get it. I'm confused too. Confused why the fuck there is also a life-size cardboard cutout of me in your closet, Breezy. And a poster. And a bunch of other stuff with my face stamped on it."

Oh God. He found her hidden trove of Westy paraphernalia. He must think she was like Blackbeard or something.

"I can explain." Her heart beat so hard that her vision was pulsing. "I can explain everything."

"Nah, don't bother." He held up a hand. "I was in your room, talking to my agent, and then my coach, about the fact that *someone* leaked the fact that I'm considering retirement. That I have a head injury and that it's caused problems. But the thing that I'm blindingly aware of is that the only person that I talked about this with was you."

"Wait . . ." Her brain tried to grasp what he was saying. "You think that I . . ." She licked her dry lips and tried again. "You think that I went to the press?"

As if on cue, her front door banged open and Neve burst in, her normally sleek ponytail gathered into an unruly messy bun. "Why aren't you answering your phone? I swear to God, I leave town to cover a few measly basketball games and everything goes to hell in a handbasket. What are you doing, Westy? First, my mom fills me that it's my little sister, then an hour ago all Twitter was in on the gig. Now, there's a shit storm brewing online with your name in the eye of." Her brow crinkled. "Is it true that you're retiring? Or is this one of those tempest-in-a-teapot rumors?"

"Don't know." Jed stared straight ahead. His phone rang again.

"You want to answer that?" Neve quizzed.

Jed shook his head. "It's my publicist again. I don't want to talk to her."

Breezy bit the inside of her cheek. He wasn't even

looking at her. The fact he knew about her fandom hidden in her closet was bad, but worse was not being entirely sure what disaster was about to come crashing down on their heads. Her tummy picked up on seismic shifts below the surface. The only question was how bad the earthquake was going to be, how much damage would occur.

"Ha." His unexpected laugh came out a sharp bark. "I got to say, I'm impressed." He gave a slow mocking clap. "You two should take this show on the road. The Angel Sisters, Live in Vegas."

"Say what?" Neve gave him one of her "shut up and speak sense" glares.

Breezy sank into a chair, her fingers grasping the armrests as if that could somehow prevent her from plummeting into the Earth's core. "You think I ratted you out, don't you?" She licked her lips, her heart beating so hard that it physically hurt. Her stomach protested. Threatened to be sick. "You think that I told your secrets to Neve."

"Not at first." Jed was granite. He'd turned to stone. His eyes were slits. No emotion registered on his face. No sign he was there at all. "But after what I found in your room. Tell me, how the hell am I supposed to believe anything from you? Was this all a lie? Something to brag about to your girlfriends? I mean, Christ, Breezy, what's the matter with you?"

"Hang on." Neve swiveled her head between them, like a spectator watching a tennis match. "I'm trying to play catch-up here, but you think my sister leaked me a tip? About what? The retirement? The head injury?"

"Everything." His tone was clipped. Flat. Final. His head didn't move even as his gaze swung to lock with hers.

"Stop, please, listen." Breezy's throat tightened. Words took effort to form. Her tongue was sluggish and clumsy. "I should have told you that I was your biggest fan. I mean, like . . . the *biggest*. But I was afraid it would freak you out, that you would think that I was interested in what this was for all the wrong reasons." Her voice cracked and it took her a moment to regain composure. "That I was wanting to be with you because who you represented, not who you actually were. But it wasn't like that. It was never like that."

"Hey, when all is said and done, I'm a simple guy. My world is black and white. And here's what I see. A woman who keeps pictures of me at her work, and hidden in her goddamn closet. A woman who sleeps with me. Gets me talking. Has me sharing private stuff that I don't tell anyone else in the world. Then she loses her job. Needs money. And check it out, she is sitting on one hell of a story scoop, one that she could cash in on." He gave a mocking pump of the fist as if opening an imaginary cash register.

"You asshole." Breezy's world went red. There was a crack. When she blinked again, she was on her feet, her palm stinging, anger radiating off her like heat on a pavement.

"Fuck." Jed clasped his jaw. "You slapped me."

"And if you say another word about my sister, I swear to the old gods and the new that your ass will be on the ground." Neve stepped to her sister's side, linking her arm. "That head injury you're apparently so worried about will feel like a tickle by the time I'm finished."

The doorbell rang again. And again. And again.

This place was like Grand Central Station.

"You've got to be kidding me." Neve groaned as a tall, blond man finally threw open the door, stood staring at them with impassive Scandinavian features.

Tor Gunnar.

Hellions coach.

A popular meme circulated around the hockey fan sites entitled The Many Faces of Tor Gunnar.

Happy: Stoic Face

Sad: Same stoic face

Hungry: Same stoic face

In Love: Same stoic face

Apparently they could add a new listing. Star Captain Announcing Surprise Retirement: Same Stoic Face.

"Quite a day." Tor's gray eyes were the color of steel at dusk.

"Thanks for getting over here," Jed said speaking fast. "I'm on my own."

"It's true then?" Tor closed the door behind him, wholesale ignoring Breezy and Neve. "Not another online rumor going wild."

"I'm considering retiring from the game. Yeah. Shit. More than considering." Jed dug his hands into his back pockets. "This is a hell of a way to break the news. I'm sorry, man. I only just decided. But—"

"Someone spilled the beans. But the source isn't in this room," Neve piped up.

There was an old saying that still waters run deep. Deep in the coach's serious eyes stirred a nameless emotion when focused on her sister.

Hard to say if he wanted to kill her or kiss her.

"This is people's lives," he bit off. "Not a game."

"I'm not dignifying that statement with a reply." Neve sniffed. "My sister had nothing to do with this. Neither did I. End of story."

"Jed . . ." Breezy knew there were right words for any occasion. She had read so many that had shaped her life, formed her worldview. But right now they all abandoned her. If only he'd look at her, but he fixed on the blank yellow wall as if the truth was written there.

And who knows, maybe it was. That wall could be spelling out a future doesn't exist.

"Come on, Westy." Tor turned for the door, shaking his head. "We can weather this at my place."

"Don't let the door hit you, Coach." Neve's tone was all sass.

He froze, his hand tightening infinitesimally on the knob before he opened it and stalked onto the porch.

"Jed." Breezy wasn't sure if she repeated the word, or if it was just the plea in her heart.

But he didn't turn back around. Didn't offer so much as a single backward glance.

He walked into the storm and when the door slammed behind all that remained was silence.

Chapter Seventeen

BREEZY SQUEEZED HER eyes shut but when she opened them her living room was still the same. Neve stood in the middle of the area rug with a "what the hell just happened" look stamped on her face.

"Before you say anything. Can I see it?" Neve crossed the room and grabbed her wrist. "The hand that decked Jed West."

"Don't try to make a joke and make me feel better." Breezy couldn't laugh, cry, sigh or even yell at her sister. How was she supposed to feel? There'd been no warning the day was going to be like this. When she woke up it had been sunny. Jed had kissed every square inch of her body. It had even been a good hair day.

No sign that the universe was sending over a giant shit storm of epic proportions.

Neve walked to the window. "He's talking to Channel Seven."

"Should you be out there?"

"Yeah. Probably. But I should be here more." She turned around. "I'm not even going to bother asking if you're okay. But seriously. What the hell? I know what Mom told me, but I want to hear it from your lips. You and Jed West got together?"

Breezy nodded miserably.

"And you didn't mention that you were his number one fan."

Breezy shook her head. Apparently head gestures were all she could muster the energy for at the moment.

Neve blew out a breath. "And he told you that he planned to retire."

More nods.

"Wow." Her sister digested the information. "He must have really trusted you, sharing information like that."

"Except now he thinks that I sold him out. Tried to cash in on the story. I get how it must look. I'm related to you, a sports journalist. I lost my job the other day. I'm worried about money. I want to open a bookshop. But I didn't say a word. I swear. Like, I think I'm falling in love with him. Real love. Not being starstruck and in lust."

Neve sank down to the floor, folded her legs crisscross applesauce, her cheeks pale. "Whoa. Okay. That's a lot to unpack. You lost your job this week? Oh my

God, Breezy. And of course you are worried about the mortgage. You just bought the cottage. And what's this about a bookshop? And sorry, you are in love with Westy?"

"Yep to all of the above." Breezy sprawled starfish on the floor beside her sister. "That about covers the situation."

"You need to tell him the truth." Her sister gripped her wrist. "That it wasn't you."

"For someone so observant, maybe you missed the whole part from a minute ago where I said that and was essentially called a liar. I'm sorry for you too. For causing more trouble between you and the coach."

Neve snorted. "Tor Gunnar? He doesn't scare me."

"Why do you guys have such beef?"

"Beef? No, no, no. Beef is delicious, especially served medium rare." She reached over and tickled her sister. "What we have is like chicken left on the counter for a week in August. Toxic. Deadly. Makes you feel sick." Her joking tone held a note of seriousness.

"But why?"

Neve's gaze locked on hers and for a moment, just a fraction, her usual confident demeanor slipped. "I have theories."

Breezy perked. "So there *is* a reason? You've never said. I just wasn't sure if Coach didn't like you in the locker room. He's youngish, but that seems old-fashioned."

"Understatement," Neve said. "But for real, there's bigger fish to fry at the moment. You dated Rory for how long? Years. You even got engaged. But you know what, in all that time, I never heard you to declare that you loved him."

"Never once?" Breezy wrinkled her brows. "Come on, are you sure?"

"Cross my heart. I wanted to bring it up when you announced the engagement, but Margot ordered me to mind my own business, said that everyone is entitled to have relationships in their own way. In her case, that means going to a remote section of Baja with two six-foot professional surfers for a getaway."

"Ah, yes." Breezy smiled in spite of herself. "You saw her last Instagram post too?"

"Her life, I swear to God." Neve shook her head. "I consider ordering a Blizzard and not doing my breakfast dishes a big free-spirited move. She's probably having a threesome in a beachside bungalow as we speak."

"Well, if she was to spare us a thought, I'm pretty sure she'd expect me to be hosting Toddler Reading Hour, not deleting my Facebook account while Jed West announces his retirement from the game."

Neve looked thoughtful. "Who is going to take his place, you think? As captain, I mean? Think Patch Donnelly is up for—hey!"

Breezy had half sat, grabbed a pillow and was now smacking her sister.

"Ouch!" Neve threw her hands over her head. "What's this for?"

"Can you not be a Hellions Angel for two seconds.

Forget he's . . . you know . . . Jed West . . . and think of him as like . . . Jed West."

Neve raised her brows. "I'm going to need help deciphering that."

"Think of him as a guy, just a guy that I am really into. Beyond all the rest of what anyone else says, least of all random strangers on the internet. Or the people out there wondering about his retirement." Breezy waved her hand in the direction of the closed up window. "I understand if it freaks him out too much that I was a huge fangirl and didn't tell him. Because that is creepy. I was creepy."

"You had a healthy fantasy."

"Yes. But all these players me and other girls drool over . . . they're like . . . people, you know? Like they are real. And he is real. And what we had, Neve, it was real and I blew it. I can't get that back."

"Can't you?" Neve looked thoughtful. "Because there might be a way."

Chapter Eighteen

FORTY-FIVE MINUTES LATER, Jed was kicked back in a patio chair on Tor's rooftop condo. "Thanks, man," he said, taking the offered pilsner. The bottle was icy cold, a welcome relief against his too-hot skin.

"Time for a come to Jesus." Tor opened his bottle with his keychain. "You've been dodging my calls since the playoffs. Now this. What the fuck?" Coach didn't raise his voice. He never did. Other coaches might scream during the game. Make themselves hoarse in the locker room. It wasn't that Tor was soft-spoken. No. There was nothing soft about Coach Gunnar. It was that he was unshakeable. Nothing rattled him.

Except for Neve Angel.

"I know. I'm sorry. Shit." Jed took a long pull from the bottle. "This isn't how I wanted it to go down, believe me. I've been trying to decide what to do for weeks."

Coach shook his head wearily. "My door has always been open to you."

"I know. I know. But I was in my head."

"And that woman." Tor turned to face out. If the Denver skyline was erased, they'd be able to look at the mountains. "The one in the little house with the big hair."

"Her name is Breezy. She's Neve Angel's little sister."

"And she ratted you out?"

"She swears she didn't. But there's that whole Occam's razor principle, right? Whatever is the simplest explanation is probably correct."

"Very logical."

"So what?" Jed's fingers clutched the bottle's neck. "You think I did the wrong thing?"

"Do you?" Coach's stare was unwavering.

Not to mention unnerving.

"Why'd she lie?" Jed got up and paced, scowled down over the railing at the pool and courtyard below. A few people swam laps or read magazines. They looked normal. Didn't they know? The world had gone mad.

"She needed the money," he continued. "She lost her job at the library. She has a mortgage. She wants to start a bookstore."

"So she was paid to do a tell-all exposé on you? By what, leaking gossip on Twitter? That'll set her up for life."

"Shit." Coach didn't say a lot, but when he did, it

always made sense. "I don't know." He raked a hand through his hair. "I'm fucking confused."

"Neve insisted her sister wasn't the leaker, I'd take that at face value."

"Say what?" Jed dropped the bottle down against his hip. "You can't stand Angel."

"That doesn't mean I have a poor opinion of her ethics," Coach shot back coolly.

Jed opened his mouth, slammed it, opened it up again and finally shrugged.

"But you don't like her."

"I don't like most people."

Jed laughed despite himself. "Fair enough." Coach was a good guy, loyal to a fault, committed to the team and had an uncanny ability to notice other people and take their measure.

"Do a gut check." Coach was big on those.

"You don't think I tried?" Jed knew his voice was sharp, but something felt broken inside him, the pieces jagged and grating. "I met this woman. It was unexpected. The connection. The attraction. It was a whirlwind. But the whole time it felt right," he quietly declared. "It felt real . . . natural even. Not a single alarm bell ever went off that she was playing me for a long-game."

"You know what? You keep talking about that girl," Tor said. "Not about retiring."

Jed froze. Shit. Coach had a point. He was mourning Breezy more than his career. He lowered his chin, glaring at his sneakers. What the hell did that mean? His phone started ringing. "Twenty bucks it's my agent."

"Or one of the guys." Tor tore the label off his bottle, rolling it neatly.

Shit. Of course. All his teammates would be seeing the retirement news pop up on their feed, or on the news. They'd be blindsided. "I'll get back to them later," he said, flicking off his phone without looking at the screen. He wanted to tune everything out.

"What'll you do now?" Tor asked. "If you don't play?"

The unsettled feeling in his stomach became turbulent. "Truthfully, I don't have the first fucking clue. I've got money. I've got time. So I'm lucky."

"Got enough rope to hang yourself."

Coach was also a "glass is half-full" type.

"I'm surprised you haven't given me shit for retiring."

Tor was quiet a moment. "I'm not happy, but from the little you've told me about your brother, I understand why you wouldn't want to push it." Tor was one of the few people in the world that he'd opened up to about Travis's injuries. Coach understood that Jed wasn't embarrassed about his brother, but wanted to look out for him, the best way he knew how. Travis coped when his world was kept quiet, with strict structure and routine. The highs couldn't get too high or the lows too low.

Nothing in Jed's career invited that.

And as Travis's condition deteriorated, any fluctuation in those routines made him increasingly agitated and erratic. And being around Jed only exasperated his own sense of loss.

"The roster's undergoing a major state of transitions," Tor continued. "Veterans are being traded. You're out. We might opt to rotate alternate captains for the moment. See who rises. Petrov might make a solid bridge to the newer players."

"Have you thought about Patch Donnelly?" The quiet new goalie had an unexpected maturity.

"Him?" Tor's brow creased. "Donnelly strings five words together on a good day."

There was that. "Focus on getting him out of his shell next season. He's a Catholic boy, right? Played at Boston College. I hear he goes to church every morning during the off-season. Petrov said he was almost a priest." Jed's muscles loosened as his brain whirled, reviewing the goalie's strengths and weaknesses.

"A good goalie lets go of fear, lives fully in the present." Tor shook his head. "He's not there. Not yet anyway. But I'll give him opportunities to prove me wrong."

Jed regarded Tor with approval. "You would have made a good general, Coach."

"Probably." Nothing else was forthcoming. Coach wasn't big on small talk or humility.

They spent the next hour drinking good beer and playing air hockey before Coach checked his watch with his usual abruptness. "Hey, I got to run. It's my night with Olive," he said by way of explanation. He shared custody of his daughter with his ex-wife and her fiancé. "I'll drop you off on the way."

"Don't worry about it, I'll Uber." But once Jed left Coach's condo, a walk sounded better. He kept to shady residential streets, crossing the road if anyone was on the sidewalk or in their front yard. It took a few times before he shook his head, laughing at himself. Not everyone was looking for him. Hell, most weren't even thinking about him.

"Paranoid much?" he muttered, shoving his hands in his pockets. His retirement from the Hellions was newsworthy, but it wasn't like he'd negotiated peace in the Middle East. Soon even the most die-hard fans would move on. Embrace the new roster. Focus on the new season.

And what would he have once the limelight faded?

More importantly, *who* would he have?

Coach had believed Breezy's denial. Jed stared up at the sunlight filtering through the maple leaves. Had he been wrong to come to a snap judgment? He'd gone into lockdown mode when he looked in that box, then remembered the closet she had steered him from the day her room flooded.

After that it was all over. He'd tried and sentenced her without letting her offer any explanation.

Kind of an asshole move, really.

No wonder she decked him. He rubbed his cheek.

The moment he'd been tested, he'd retreated. Freaked out. Acted like a coward.

Bitterness flooded his mouth.

Maybe she'd called? Maybe he should nut up and call her. He turned on his phone, checking his voice mail. By the time the screen powered on, he'd made a decision. He'd dial her up, ask to meet and talk things over. She deserved that much.

There were four new voice mails. Two from his agent. One from his publicist. But it was the third name on the list that froze the blood in his veins.

"Shit." It was like someone Windexed the grime off his brain and the truth shown.

His arm holding the phone, dropped limply to his side. The street might not even exist.

He'd gotten everything wrong. Royally screwed the pooch.

No, those were just statements of fact. They didn't come close to describing his fuck up. He'd just crashed and burned so hard that he should be nothing but a few splinters of bone, some singed hair. He resumed walking, picking up the pace, as if he could move faster than the avalanche of regret bearing down on him.

Breezy hadn't done shit. And he'd accused her with all the self-righteousness of an Old Testament God. He could barely focus. His body ached to move. Run. But even as his feet pounded the concrete, breath tearing from his chest, a single question chased him.

What the hell was he going to do now?

Chapter Nineteen

FOR THE NEXT few days, social media had a field day with the news of Jed's surprise retirement. His image was everywhere, in the form of career montages and old interview clips. Every time she glimpsed his face it punched another hole in Breezy's stomach.

It was impossible to venture online or read a paper. Instead, Breezy tried to find solace in her favorite place on Earth—her bed. But even reading eluded her. She was unable to escape into make-believe.

This wasn't a book slump. It was a bone-crushing pain.

After a busy morning talking to real estate agents and visiting banks and putting together the first stage of her plan, she went to her closet and yanked out the cardboard Jed West cutout.

"Why don't you call me?" she snapped.

He stared at a fixed point with that stupidly perfect smile.

"Look. I can't call *you*. Not when you're so mad at me. The last thing I want to do is have you not believe me."

She sighed.

"I know. I lied to you, or at least hung out in that gray area of omission. I guess that I felt stupid if you knew I was a fan. I was afraid you'd dismiss me, or think I was desperate. A pathetic bookworm who believes in fairy tales and fantasizes about a prince. Actually . . . it's sort of our story, but it's more than that. Just like you are more than the guy everyone cheers for on game nights."

She dabbed the corner of her eyes. "Anyway, speaking of pathetic, I should stop having a long one-sided discussion with a piece of sexy cardboard." She regarded the cutout for a long moment before making a decision. "This will hurt me more than it will hurt you."

She marched to the kitchen and yanked a garbage bag from the roll beneath the sink. Back in her bedroom, she folded the cutout in half and stuck the sucker inside. The poster met the same fate as did her calendar, the Westy bobblehead and other assorted trinkets.

It wasn't that she wanted to trash Jed, just to bid a firm farewell to the time of her life that had loved the myth more than the man.

The part that no longer existed.

Outside her window, an old Jeep Wagoneer parked. Neve's car. Breezy drew in a ragged breath as her sister climbed out of the SUV and strode up the front yard with her purposeful gait, fear retreated.

"Hey girl." Her sister came through the front door. "Ready to go? We have a big day."

"First up, party," Breezy said. She had to compartmentalize if she wanted to make it through everything they had planned.

"Then podcast," Never concluded firmly. "Let's go."

Breezy was going to make an announcement at Granny Dee's ninetieth birthday party. And later, an announcement of a different variety.

But she couldn't think about that yet, not if she didn't want to pass out from nerves.

When she and Neve entered Aunt Shell's house, the party was in full swing. The living room filled with people as well as ninety purple glitter balloons, Granny Dee's favorite color. Breezy waited until the end of dinner before hitting her wineglass with a fork.

"Everyone? Can I have your attention?"

The banter and discussions faded as all gazes swung in her direction. She wiggled her toes in her wedge sandals. Center stage had never been a place where she felt confident.

"Um." She cleared her throat. "We're all gathered here today to celebrate the long life of an amazing woman—"

"It's not my funeral yet, dear," Granny piped up from the head of the table. "Remember I intend to live to one hundred and ten. That leaves me a good twenty more years."

"No one in the room disbelieves you, Granny. And want to know why? Because you are like a fine wine." Breezy lifted her glass in toast. "Getting better and better with age."

"Damn straight." Granny glugged the rest of her glass.

"But I want you to know that you have helped influence me. As a kid, heck, even as an adult, I wasn't known for my self-confidence. But you have always encouraged me to live my best self. Be my best truth. That's why I wanted to share exciting news. Many of you know that after an amazing run, I was let go from the library. It could have really been a kick in the gut. In fact, it was for a time. But then I remembered a line from *The Sound of Music*, a movie that I used to watch every Easter with Granny."

"You know it! That Captain von Trapp makes my hills come alive." Granny gave a shoulder shimmy while two of the uncles covered their ears.

"In the film, Maria learns that when a door closes, somewhere a window opens. Well, I wanted to share that I found my window."

She reached into her purse and pulled out a manila folder. Her shoulders rose and fell with the deep breath. "Okay. Here goes nothing." She removed the logo she'd gotten designed this morning and held it aloft.

"What is it?" Granny adjusted her spectacles, leaning forward.

"It looks like a bookstore." Her mother peered with a slight frown. "You're going to work at a shop?"

"I'm going to own the shop," Breezy said, her voice quiet but unwavering. "Itsy Bitsy Children's Books. I'm signing the lease. We're just negotiating the contract with the bank."

"Let me have a look." Granny reached for the plans. She perused them for a long minute before giving a nod of approval. "This looks wonderful, Bumper Butt. Really good stuff. See, being a bookworm can be good business."

It was clear she directed the pointed comment at Breezy's mom, who didn't respond, merely gathered dirty dishes the rest of the room was back to talking, laughing and drinking.

BREEZY WATCHED HER mom walk out and despite everything, her Granny's beaming face, her sister's thumbs-up, it hurt with a calculated paper cut sting.

After ten minutes her mom hadn't returned. Her empty space in the room loomed large.

She was too old to need her mother's approval, but that didn't mean she didn't want it. Her whole life she'd felt like she let her mom down. Now, here she was, a small business owner. And still nothing? The disappointment in her belly filled with another emotion, anger. She wasn't Neve, but come on.

She drained her wineglass and with a belly full of liquid courage, walked into the kitchen. She was a princess and this wasn't her only dragon to slay today.

But Mom wasn't there.

Breezy looked around. Did she ghost?

There was the sound of footsteps on the steps and door creaked open. Mom emerged holding a bouquet of yellow-and-pink flowers.

"Honey," she said, breathless. "For you. I ran down to the corner flower shop in these shoes. I can't believe I didn't snap a heel. It's like I always say, better to pay for quality."

"You got these?" Breezy slowly reached out and took the bouquet. "Really?"

"I'm not good talking about my feelings. But I want you to know how proud I am of you. You did it. You really did it this time."

Breezy stared, stunned. Had she choked on a piece of birthday cake because it sounded like Mom was expressing pride. In fact, she was tearing up despite the fact she wore mascara and expertly applied eyeliner.

"I know that there were times when I wanted you to be more like . . . me . . . rather than like you. After you lost your job, and right after you bought the house, I was worried. I'd even spoke to Jim about cashing in on a CD to help you with the mortgage. I was going to tell you today."

"Thank you, Mom. Really. But that's not going to be necessary. I've got a good loan, but the fact you wanted to help me means the world."

"Itsy Bitsy Books. What a cute name."

Breezy gave a small shy smile. "You used to sing me

the "Itsy Bitsy Spider" when I was little, remember? And you'd always tickled me when singing the 'down came the rain' part."

"To hear you laugh. You had those dimples. Oh, and that adorable laugh. This new step has taken courage and guts. I've been wrong to dismiss you. Wrong to think that you were settling. Granny won't admit it now, but when I was younger, she thought my dream of figure skating was unrealistic. She advised me to go to secretarial school."

"Really?"

"Yes." Mom grimaced. "Trust me. She's mellowed with age. Your aunts could tell stories that would turn your hair gray. But never mind that. Let it go and let it be."

"That's very Buddha of you."

"Therapy. It's a new thing that I'm trying. I just want you to know that I am proud of you. That I don't always have the words, but there is love for you here." She pressed a hand over her chest. "And you can bet that Itsy Bitsy is going to be a success."

"You really think so?"

"Honey, you're my daughter. Once you find your passion, you chase it and let nothing get in your way."

Breezy bent and breathed in the blossoms, they smelled sweet and fresh, like hope.

Chapter Twenty

Breezy still had one more dragon to slay if she wanted a shot at getting her fairy tale.

"Where do you want to do this?" she asked her sister that night, after they got back to her cottage following Granny's party.

"Let's try your kitchen table."

Once seated, Neve got out her audio recorder. After some fiddling, she nodded. "Ready, Freddy."

Breezy reached for her glass of water and took a long sip.

"You don't have to do this," Neve repeated for what must be the thousandth time.

"No. I do." Breezy took one more gulp. Her stomach hurt. Talking was scary, but it was the only way. If Jed didn't want to listen to her talk, she had to veer from usual channels, because at the end of the day, having a deep and meaningful talk with cardboard Jed wasn't going to accomplish anything.

If he heard her words maybe they'd burrow into his heart and put down roots. Help him believe her. Help him realize that what they shared was beyond anything she knew leading up to it.

"Okay I'm ready when you are." Neve fingered the record button.

"Let's do it."

Neve leaned in. "Hello and welcome to another edition of *Sports Heaven*, with me, Neve, Denver's favorite Angel, although once you get a load of my special guest that could be up for debate.

"Lots happening the past few days in Hockeylandia, namely the huge shake-up on the Hellions roster with Captain Jed West announcing a sudden retirement from the game. Unconfirmed sources cite the reason is due to a health issue, likely a cumulative of head injuries and a desire to leave the sport to proactively protect his handsome noggin.

"Predictably, this has kicked up quite the fuss among pundits about the dangers of CTE or chronic traumatic encephalopathy, a progressive degenerative disease of the brain found primarily in athletes with a track record for repetitive brain trauma like concussions or repeated blows to the head.

"But throughout the story, another person has slipped into the spotlight. A woman who was with Jed when the news broke out. An ordinary woman who has weathered an extraordinary situation of media and scrutiny.

"A woman who I'm proud to call my sister." Neve blew her a kiss. "Thanks for talking with me today, Breezy," she said.

"Uh. Hi." Breezy leaned in and spoke to the mic like it might jump up and bite her on the chin.

"Never expected to have you on my show."

"That makes two of us." An awkward silence lingered. Breezy's blood pressure began to creep up, her cheeks flushing as a tight band of pressure spread across her chest.

"Listeners out there might appreciate hearing how you're *a yuuuge* hockey fan. Want to fill people in about the Hellions Angels?"

Breezy started off a little slow, unsure and mumbling as she shared how the Angel women love the game and it has become the compass in their family, the one thing they can all agree on.

"So true," Neve laughed. "I don't normally get personal on here, but I think it's fair to say that hockey is the glue that holds our family together. Why, I don't even see you guys much during the off-season." She leaned in, her face getting serious. "This is funny stuff, but you're on the show for a more serious reason. You were in a relationship with Jed and he thinks you are the leaker of the story. So today it's time to set the record straight."

"I hope so."

"Did you leak information about Jed's condition to me or any other member of the press?"

"No." Her voice was husky so she paused, cleared her throat and tried again. "Sorry, no. I never spoke about it to anyone. That was his business. His health. I'd never betray that trust."

"Over the last few weeks you've developed certain feelings for Westy, is that correct?"

"Yes. Since he joined the Hellions, I always had what you could call a crush. I mean, I have two eyes, and he is gorgeous. Plus, I was attracted to his talent and, most of all, that and his sportsmanship."

"Then you had an opportunity to meet him?"

"I did. He came and filled in at my library as a special guest. Through a series of . . . unfortunate events, we ended up spending time together. I got to know him as a man. And I realized that he wasn't a beautiful face. He has a beautiful heart. He is even better than what you see on television. He's kindhearted. He is funny. And he made me believe that I could be better. That I could reach out for my goals and achieve them."

"If you had something to say to Jed right now, what would it be?"

"I'd tell him that I am in love with him. With *him*. Not the image. Not the fame. Not the hockey. With the man he is down to his bones. And that . . . that I'm sorry—so sorry—that I was embarrassed about my fangirling. That I hid the truth from you because it made

me scared you would think that I had ulterior motiva-
tions. It was a stupid choice that only ended up doing
exactly what I was afraid of, making you feel like I was
a phony puck bunny concocting a devious plan. Nothing could be further from the truth. I love you and if
you are listening, I hope that you believe me. Because
it's my truth."

When she looked up Neve had tears in her eyes. She
reached over and took her hand and gave it a squeeze
before saying, "Wow. Powerful stuff. And I'll let you
know that my sister is honest. She says what she means.
If she said that she loves you, Jed, that means that you
can take that information to the bank and cash it. The
question remains now, will you take her at her word?
The puck's in your net, buddy. And that's it for our special edition. Now it remains to be seen if true love can
win the day."

She clicked off. "Now what?"

Breezy forced a smile that she didn't feel. It was taking
every inch of her willpower not to rock in a corner or
chew her nails down to nubs. "Now we wait."

JED HAD FLASHBACKS as he got off the plane from Oakland. Not again. During the short duration of his flight,
his phone had apparently blown up like he was Batman
on Devil's Night in Gotham. He sat down in an empty
chair at the gate and checked what the hell was going
on. Every message and voice mail said the same thing.

Check the *Sports Heaven* Facebook page.

He listened to Neve's podcast on occasion. It was part of the reason he'd agreed to sit down for her interview at Zachary's a couple of weeks ago. The first step on what led him on the wild journey to Breezy. She was known for blunt opinions. And this time, he could only guess that she'd put his nuts on the chopping block for blowing off her sister.

The past two nights he'd almost called Breezy at least three dozen times. But he had to go to San Francisco. See his brother. Talk to Tamara. Set a few things straight. And what he needed to say to Breezy wasn't going to cut it over the phone. She needed to be in front of him. He needed to look her in the eyes.

But as he clicked to the podcast, listening to her halting declaration, his heart turned inside out. His brave, brave girl. What she'd done took guts and all he could do now was hope to live up to the challenge of being worthy of her.

As he walked through the Denver terminal he grew aware of eyes on him. It wasn't unusual. Being who he was meant he always had people staring. Usually a request for photographs. But this time was different. People were . . . clapping.

"What are you waiting for? Go get her!" an older woman shouted, walking out of a smoothie shop.

"Need a lift?" A driver pulled over on a motorized cart, tipping his hat. "On the house."

"Thanks, man." Jed jumped on, grateful at least that he'd packed light. No baggage.

Someone whistled. "Don't let us down, Westy," a dude in a camo shirt shouted from a bar, raising a nearly empty Bloody Mary.

"I'll do my best," he called back to cheers.

A shit-eating grin stretched from ear to ear. He'd never been one to wear his heart on his sleeve. But right now it was bursting out of his chest like a damn cartoon character. If he could, he'd hire a frigging skywriter, or singing telegram, or buy out a florist, or all three. But he didn't have time.

He had himself and had to hope that would be enough.

Because he'd been an ass.

The driver refused to let him jump out once they left the gates, insisted on taking him all the way to long-term parking.

"I've been married thirty-nine years and we've had our ups and downs, but know what we've always had? Passion. When you've got that, everything else can go."

He refused the tip.

At Breezy's place, it was Neve who answered the door. "Get in," she ordered, shutting the door behind her as she stepped onto the porch. "Now, let's get a few ground rules straight."

"Or what, you'll slap me too?"

She didn't crack a smile. "My sister put it all on the

line for you. Make her a public laughingstock and what she did will feel like a gentle caress."

"Hey. I can take it from here." Breezy stood in the doorway, clutching a mug.

Neve forked her fingers into a V-shape and raised them to her eyes before slipping them around and poking his chest. "I'm watching you."

"Neve!" Breezy yelped. "Thank you. That's enough."

"Love you, sis. You need anything, anything at all give a holler."

With a "peace out" gesture, she was gone.

They were alone.

"Can I come in?"

Breezy nodded, stepping aside to let him enter. Her hands trembled. "So you heard the podcast? I'm sorry, I know I must have put you in an awkward position."

"Never apologize. You were amazing. Correction. You *are* amazing. And I'm an idiot who doesn't deserve you."

She visibly exhaled.

"So you're saying that you believe me?"

"I wasn't thinking straight. I got scared. Scared that you didn't see me. That you didn't want *me*. That you only were interested in Westy. I wish you had told me the truth up front, but I get why you didn't . . . why you couldn't. Because my life is a lot. Like what happened in the past few days." He took a breath. "It was my sister-in-law. Tamara, by the way. Travis's wife. She's the one who talked."

Breezy's eyes opened wide at his admission. "She leaked to the press?"

"My brother's condition has deteriorated. It's fucking sad. And I've been so focused on the season, and then my own condition, that I was out of reach. She felt alone. Abandoned. I'd sent money, but I've always deposited it into an account that he had access to and turned out he went on a wild gambling binge. Spent everything. They were broke and she hasn't had a great relationship with my parents for years. They shut down hard after Travis was injured and she's felt abandoned. I had called her and let slip to Travis about my condition. He told her and in a moment of desperation, she went to the press, hoping to sell my retirement as a scoop to one of the tabloids. It didn't work but the legitimate press got wind of it and . . . well, you know what happened.

"That's where I've been the last few days. I had to get out there and make sure my brother was set up. And I worked things out with Tamara. She's had a hard time, more than any of us could imagine. But I've committed to paying off their house and setting up a college fund for my nephew. I have been blessed with more money than any one man needs to be comfortable and helping ease her burden and stress is the right thing to do. She was sorry and I believe her. I've never had to walk in her shoes."

She was quiet a long moment. "Did you see your brother?"

Jed shook his head. "He doesn't want to. I'm hoping

that someday that will change, but for now I have to respect his wishes. He doesn't have a lot left. The least he can do is determine his company. I spoke to doctors and they suspect it's full-blown CTE." His Adam's apple bobbed as if swallowing came with great difficulty. "It's such complete bullshit. He never did anything wrong. All he did was play a game. That's all. Fuck. He was just a kid. It's not fair. Why wasn't it me?"

"I'm sorry." Breezy set her mug on a table and as she walked toward him, the strangeness between them dissipated, as if blown away by an invisible wind. She couldn't help his brother, but she could help this man in front of her.

"Breezy." He whispered her name like a prayer and then she was there, wrapping her arms around him and pulling him close. And for a moment, he was able to let go of the grief that had been crushing him. It was easier when she offered to help share the load. It didn't pay to be the strong, silent type when it came to being in a relationship.

And it was time he admitted he needed backup. He glanced down at her, curls pinned back beneath that polka-dot headband. In her own steady way, she was better than a princess. She was a Viking shield maiden. "I'm so sorry that I didn't believe you."

"Don't worry about it. I didn't make it easy," she said ruefully.

"But I should have because I love you, Breezy Angel."

His lips brushed hers as his hands migrated to his favorite place on Earth, the dip in her waist.

"You do?" She breathed against him, a tremble in her voice.

"So fucking much. And I'm never going to get tired of telling you. I want to be the one who makes you believe in fairy tales."

"You do, and I love you for it." She wrapped her arm around his neck. "And I've just thought of the perfect book for you."

"That a fact?"

"Have you ever read *The NeverEnding Story*?"

"No." He nipped her lower lip. "But I'm liking the sound of it."

Chapter Twenty-One

. . . a month later

"THIS IS THE last one." Jed sauntered into the bedroom with a cardboard box. "And I got to say, if owning too many shoes was a crime, you'd be staring down a life sentence without the possibility of parole."

She peered up from the bottom drawer that she had half filled with jeans. "'I have too many shoes' is something no girl has said ever. Besides, didn't hear any complaints last night."

"When you stripped down to your stilettos?" He gripped his chest and pretended to stagger. "Remember that I'm recovering from a head injury, a weak man."

"Mmm-hmm." She erased the smile from her lips and crawled onto his king-size bed, reaching for her phone. "On that note, I have an idea."

He set down the box next to his walk-in closet and collapsed next to her. "What are you up to now?"

"Just jumping onto Amazon to order a dirty nurse costume," she answered with studied nonchalance.

He gave a lazy chuckle. "Sounds good."

"What do you think of this one?" She held up the screen. The dress was short, white and barely covered the model's nipples let alone her hoo-ha. "Comes with a garter belt, but stocking sold separately."

"What?" His eyes flew open in surprise. "You're being serious?"

"As a heart attack." She activated her one-click finger while setting her features to an expression of mock concern. "After all, snookum, if we're going to be living together, then you're going to have to accept a few things. Like the fact that I plan on looking after you." She finger-walked her hand over to the gap between his khaki shorts and worn gray shirt, swirling her finger around his belly muscle. Her chest burbled with a repressed moan as he automatically flexed from the gentle tickle, revealing a ladder of muscle.

Quick as a wink, he grabbed her hand. But rather than coaxing her to keep up the dirty, flirty fun, he laced his fingers with hers, lifted her hand to his lips and planted a gentle kiss between the knuckles. "You happy about having a new change of address? I know how much having your own place meant to you."

He was fishing, and it was adorable. "It did. And still does. But Margot's coming back and needs a place. The timing is going to work out perfectly. Bonus points for the fact that I can playact being the mean old landlady." She gave her chin a musing rub. "I should stick a no-threesome clause in her contract. Remember there's that church at the end of my street, she is liable to give the congregation a heart attack. Or start deflowering all the virgins."

"Your friend sounds adventurous."

"Hey now!" She smacked him with a giggle. "Don't get any fresh ideas, Don Juan. I don't plan on sharing."

"Hell no. I've got my hands full right here." He rolled her onto her side and pressed up behind, the big spoon to her little. He planted a shiver-inducing kiss behind one ear. "Heart too."

She wiggled back against him. "I think the coach idea might be great. You are good at building people up."

It was one of the post-retirement ideas that floated his way. The University of Denver hockey team needed a new coach. The timing was right. He'd be going in next week to have a sit-down and learn more. Staying connected to the game had appeal, the idea of quitting cold turkey didn't sit right. Besides, he genuinely liked helping people work hard to find their best self.

"You got to stop being cute or how am I ever going to finish packing. I also need to review the winter stock order." Itsy Bitsy Books was making a name for itself, the clientele growing by the week.

"Hey. I want to take you up to the mountains tonight. After you get everything done for the shop. What do you say? We can stay in an old hotel and spend tomorrow hiking, skinny-dipping in lakes."

"Brrrr, that sounds chilly," she murmured, unwilling to stretch her mind beyond the comfort of his arms, this perfect cozy moment.

"Don't worry." He nuzzled her neck. "I'll keep you warm."

"This is going to take some getting used to." She hesitated, keeping her gaze trained on the charm bracelet she kept twisting on her wrist.

"What's up?" He smoothed the worry lines cutting the space between her brows.

"My life used to be ordinary. Get up at seven. Work. Home. Netflix. Read. Repeat." She glanced over one shoulder. "Like that was my day. I wasn't a gal who wore stilettos and nothing else. And certainly didn't head out to hike for the weekend. But deep down, I had that potential. *You* saw that in me, Jed. Things that I hadn't known about myself. Things no one else noticed. You found parts of me that I didn't know existed."

He gave a slow nod. "That feeling goes both ways. I was going adrift and everything in my life was about to change. You saw me for more than the game, more than the player. And that anchored me."

They shared a long, sweet kiss before she pulled back, pressing her forehead to his. "So . . . about this whole walking on trails in the mountains idea. Why not? Life is short and everything that I never do, I want to start doing with you."

"I can't promise you an easy life, or perfection, but I can promise to give this relationship my all, because the difference between extraordinary and ordinary is that little bit of extra."

"I'll always go the extra mile." He braced her face in between his big hands, tilting her head back for a kiss. His lips covered hers as he breathed into her mouth. "You're nothing ordinary, Breezy Angel. You're my game changer."

Can't wait for more of the
Hellions Angels? Coach Tor and
Neve Angel's steamy standoff is up next in

HEAD COACH

Coming November 2017!

About the Author

LIA RILEY is a contemporary romance author. *USA Today* describes her as "refreshing" and *RT Book Reviews* calls her books "sizzling and heartfelt." She loves her husband, three kids, wandering redwood forests and a perfect pour over coffee. She is 25% sarcastic, 54% optimistic, and 122% bad at math (good thing she writes happy endings for a living). She and her family live mostly in Northern California.

Discover great authors, exclusive offers, and more at hc.com.

A Letter from the Editor

Dear Reader,

I hope you liked the latest romance from Avon Impulse! If you're looking for another steamy, fun, emotional read, be sure to check out some of our upcoming titles.

If you're a fan of historical romance, get excited! We have two new novellas from beloved Avon authors coming in August. JUST ANOTHER VISCOUNT IN LOVE by Vivienne Lorret is a charming story about an unlucky-in-love Viscount who just wants to find a wife. But every lady he pursues ends up married to another . . . until he meets Miss Gemma Desmond and he vows not to let this woman slip through his fingers! This is a delightful, witty story that will appeal to any/all historical romances fans—even if you've never read Viv before!

We also have a fabulous new story from Lorraine Heath! GENTLEMEN PREFER HEIRESSES is a new story in her Scandalous Gentlemen of St. James series. The second son of a Duke has no reason to give up his wild ways and marry, but when an American heiress catches his eye, the prospect of marriage seems much more appealing. As any true #Heathen (a Lorraine Heath superfan!) knows, her books are deeply emotional and always end with a glorious HEA. This novella is no different!

Never fear contemporary romance fans . . . we didn't forget about you! Tracey Livesay is back at the end of August with LOVE WILL ALWAYS REMEMBER, a fun and sexy new novel with a While You Were Sleeping spin! When a woman awakens from a coma with no memories from the past six years, she's delighted to learn a handsome, celebrity chef is her fiancée . . . or is he? Don't miss this wonderful diverse romance that will have you sighing with happiness!

You can purchase any of these titles by clicking the links above or by visiting our website, www. AvonRomance.com. Thank you for loving romance as much as we do . . . enjoy!

> *Sincerely,*
> *Nicole Fischer*
> *Editorial Director*
> *Avon Impulse*

He had nothing more to prove in the sport, not to critics. Not even to his fucking father. He'd persevered until he'd won everything there was to win. But now he had a neurology appointment set for a few days from today.

And if and when he made a decision about next season, he didn't want that moment to happen in the vicinity of the noisiest journalist in Denver.

Breezy switched gears. No more Madonna. Now she was belting out the chorus from a vaguely familiar musical.

His phone buzzed with a text. Coach.

Tor Gunnar: *Beers and air hockey this afternoon?*

He and Tor had been getting friendlier over the past season. They had enough in common. Two single guys. Didn't poke into each other's private lives. Talked strategy. Kept it easy.

It was cool, except he didn't want easy right now.

Jed West: *Busy*

Tor Gunnar: *Too bad. Angel's got hold of my number and calling me on speed dial. Wants a fucking quote on the contract negotiations.*

Jed West: *Why not give her something?*

Tor Gunnar: *I need to feed a jackal like I need a third nut.*

Jed smirked, turning off his phone. He didn't want to think about a lockout. Or what Tor would say if he knew he had Neve's sister sprawled naked in his bed.

He plated their breakfasts. The sun beamed through

the kitchen window, warming the back of his neck. His shoulders relaxed. He liked this, being normal, fixing waffles for a woman, listening to her terrible singing, knowing that once they finished the meal he'd coat her luscious body with whipped cream and devour second breakfast.

This wasn't just a bit of fun on the side. She'd slipped by his defenses and gotten under his skin in a way no woman ever had. It was a problem, but maybe a good one. To be with Breezy was to take a chance, but if he wanted something new in his life, he had to be willing to do what he'd never done.

THIS WAS THE best weekend of her life. Breezy never believed the idea that hurting could also feel good, but the soreness between her legs was nothing short of delicious.

Turned out Jed had a bit of a kinky side, loved watching them in his big mirror. He'd bent her over his dresser, driving hard and fast from behind, palming her breasts with one hand while working over her slick clit with the other. It was like having an out-of-body experience, watching the scene unfold. And as she gazed at her reflection—she didn't look pathetically grateful, or insecure. She looked . . . hot, sexy even. Mouth swollen. Eyes bright with lust.

Was that line of thinking even allowed? Could she talk that way about herself without sounding conceited?

She never tried before. With a deep breath, she had let the word creep into her psyche.

Hey, I look hot. Whoa. I look fucking hot.

Her lips were swollen from kissing, skin flushed from Jed's beard. Her hair had gone absolutely hog wild, but the look was less finger-in-a-light-socket-meets-hurricane and more bow-chica-wow-wow-honey-dip-chocolate-chip-shoop-shoop-de-doop.

God, yes. She gathered the sheets to her chest and giggled. This was as close to perfect as life could be.

"Tell me a secret." He paused in rubbing almond oil into the soles of her feet.

"A secret?" She frowned, considering. "What kind?"

"One no one else knows." He tickled the arch of her foot.

"Hmm." There was one. She hadn't even spilled the beans to Neve or Margot. Or barely even admitted it to herself. But every Sunday night, as she cleaned her cottage for the coming week, bracing herself for the tedious onslaught from Tater Tots and the fear that at last would come the announcement that funding was dried up and she was out of a job, there *was* a dream.

She traced her tongue along the back of her front teeth. It was hard to get the words out. But come on, here she was, curled up in bed beside Jed West and even though she had started thinking about him less and less as Jed West, hockey god and more and more as just Jed, the expert Belgian waffle-making cuddler. This very act was proof positive evidence that dreams could come true.

And all those stars she'd wished upon when she was younger, the wordless pleas to be able to skate, to make her mom proud, that had all fallen on deaf cosmic ears finally made sense. The universe had been saving up its blessings to rain them down over her in one glorious torrent.

"Open a bookshop." There. The words were out now, no take backs. "A children's bookshop. Stock everything from picture books to young adult."

Jed paused, considering. Nothing in his face suggested that he thought her idea was funny. "Makes sense." He went back to rubbing her feet.

"What? That was it? That's the sum total of your reaction," she asked. "This is a deep, dark secret. One that I've never told a living soul. And look at you."

"What about me?" He frowned, scrubbing his beard.

"You're acting as surprised as if I'd announced that ketchup tastes good on French fries."

"What do you want me to say?" His gaze went strangely tight. "What do you want me to say? You're a children's librarian."

"So?"

"So." His dark brows rose fractionally. "That means you like books."

"Yes, but . . ." She didn't know why she wanted to argue against her dream. Maybe because he made it sound too simple and straightforward. Too possible.

Grrrr.

But Jed didn't have to stress out over making his